A Dying

of

Starlight

To friends, fairytales, and foolishness

Content warnings on final page

Sacrifice

The Last Princess of Rosenly

The last princess of Rosenly will never get any wishes, but if she had one, she'd wish for people to stop mentioning her impending death.

This might seem impractical to some—to wish for a tragedy to be silenced instead of avoided—but the last princess of Rosenly learned long ago that nothing good ever comes from wishing for more life. Especially when that life's meant to be hers.

The princess reaches up with thin, bone-strung fingers. She brushes an errant black clump of hair behind her shoulder just as the gates begin to open, recoiling when her skin makes contact with a tendril of light. Though the princess hadn't felt it slip, her mother leans over to straighten her tiara.

Princesses—or at least, princesses like her—need to be beautiful. Princesses—or at least, princesses like her—have their every imperfection hidden away beneath layers of silk and powder that are then more carefully guarded than any palace wall or precious stone ever has been.

The last princess of Rosenly doesn't look the way princesses are meant to. Her skin—once an even richer brown than her father's—began to dull around her thirteenth birthday and has only worsened since. Her once pampered, meticulously curled hair now pools like ink stains in the hollow indents around her collarbone where fat and muscle once sat. Sometimes, when she's alone, the princess twists her neck until she can fit her jaw into the sunken pocket left behind, letting bone interlock with bone and engrossing herself in the morbid fantasy of what might happen if her shoulder moved only slightly further back.

The last princess of Rosenly has been more death than girl since her very creation, but now, as her end grows nearer, she wears it as visibly as a fur-lined cloak.

Almost reflexively, the last princess of Rosenly tugs at the edge of her sleeve. A failing body is an imperfection most suitors are willing to overlook. There's a certain appeal to smallness, after all; a sensuality to a partner with a snappable spine. But death is the lesser of the last Princess of Rosenly's physical imperfections. Beneath her skin lay thousands of pinpricks of light, eternally shifting and swirling no matter how desperately she attempts to will them to tranquility. Her dark hair's filled with strands of glowing white, and there's an unmistakable, unnatural shine around her honey-brown eyes.

The Last Princess of Rosenly's body is a tapestry of ever-present reminders that she's been a monstrosity since birth and that the moment her next birthday arrives, the skies will descend to reclaim her.

Light too can be alluring, though. To some. There's a certain exclusivity in being able to call something monstrous your own. Her maids alternate between leaving her arms bare or covered each kissing line to maximize her potential appeal.

The princess much prefers full-sleeved days.

The gates finish opening. The princess rolls her shoulders back and straightens her spine. She does her best to not look at her fingers.

There was once a time when the last princess of Rosenly looked forward to kissing lines. They'd been less frequent when she was younger, and she'd been filled with all the naivety that came along with being royal-born. It had been easier to forget the taste of a foreign mouth against hers in the in-betweens when she'd had more time to recuperate. More than that, though, was the sense of hope they always used to bring. Were she still naive, the princess might crane her neck to try and pick out which stranger in the crowd would be the one to save her, half-convinced she'd know exactly who it was the moment their eyes met.

(The Last Princess of Rosenly was raised on fairy tales, of course. They were her birthright)

Now, she sits straight because it's polite to. Now, she smiles because strangers don't kiss princesses who don't smile.

Now, she's avoiding looking at her skin.

In the minuscule part of her brain that still yearns for wishes, the last princess of Rosenly's hoping not for a knowing glance or a heroic kiss, but simply that the first person in line doesn't get too visibly upset about her dying.

The first kisser is summoned. She looks to be nearing her late-thirties which might have once offended the princess, but she exhausted all the more age-appropriate suitors well before reaching fifteen.

The woman's clothes are brown and plain. Her hair is brown and simple. She doesn't even attempt to meet the princess's gaze as she approaches the throne, and were she to try, the Last Princess of Rosenly already knows that the contact would set nothing alight within her chest.

"Good morning," the princess nods. "Thank you f—"

The woman falls to her knees. The princess tightens her smile. This will be a crier, then.

The kisser chokes out prayers and apologies that the last princess of Rosenly does her best to react appropriately to. Eventually, the stranger rises on shaking legs. Thick snot dribbles down to cling at her chin, but the princess holds out her right hand regardless and waits for it to be kissed.

(It's less improper, of course, for a commoner to kiss a princess once they've already kissed her knuckles)

The woman kisses her right hand. The woman kisses her left. Then and only then does the last princess of Rosenly give in to the exhaustion at her shoulders and lean forward. The woman tastes of salt, mucus, and skin—always skin. The princess hates the skin more than the mucus, somehow—and her tears burn against deep cracks in eternally chapped lips. The princess feels a tongue press against her mouth and parts it slightly before letting her eyes fall shut.

(This is her favourite part of kissing, of course: getting to finally close her eyes)

And then, it's done. The woman draws away and the princess can already sense her failure in her mother's ever-tapping foot. Still, she slowly raises her hand to check for herself, just in case.

(Hope is a very hard thing to kill in a princess, after all)

She's met with swirling specks of yellow and white and the harsh reminder that she's still living on borrowed time.

The Last Princess of Rosenly fixes her spine once again. "Thank you," she says.

"And you," the stranger whispers. She never did get a name. They rarely do.

And then, she's gone and replaced with a man whose beard scrapes against the princess's chin. And then, he's gone and replaced with another stranger whose tongue presses just a little too hard.

The Last Princess of Rosenly tells herself she turns off her mind at some point during each kissing line. This is inaccurate. It's hard to stop thinking with your life on the line and a foreign muscle at your molars. She doesn't block out the line so much as she falls into it. A constant slew of faces she'll never remember and breath and tears and snot. A never-ending, unbreakable intrusion that sets her body so on edge that the specifics of who exactly's facilitating it cease to matter.

And then, there's a girl.

'Girl' isn't quite accurate, the princess supposes, for she stopped considering herself one ages ago, and if anything, this stranger seems slightly older than her. But there is a less-than-adult woman with dark hair and dark eyes and her fists shoved into pant pockets.

There is a less-than-adult-woman wearing *pants*.

Perhaps she's new to Rosenly. Maybe she's unused to the customs of kissing lines. Perhaps, even, she's from someplace far, far away where princesses get to be real and solid and living.

The Last Princess of Rosenly sits up slightly taller. For the first time in months, she's overwhelmed by the urge to wipe at her mouth; filled with a sudden want to protect this less-than-adult from the remnants of those who came before her.

The princess doesn't move her arm, of course. Princesses worthy of saving don't get to cringe at a stranger's spit.

There hasn't been a less-than-adult in the kissing line for years now. That has to mean something.

The Last Princess of Rosenly feels it and hates it instantly, yet feels it all the same: the swell of possibility. Unshakable eagerness at the chance of surviving this.

(Hope is a very hard thing to kill in a princess, after all)

The Last Princess of Rosenly has been told very little about the stars, but she's somehow certain that if they do have any control over who her true love will be, this is exactly how they'd do it.

A stranger in pants who's come almost too late.

The stranger steps forward. She's staring at The Last Princess of Rosenly's eyes before the princess even finishes looking up, and when their gazes meet, it happens. The princess feels it; not a spark nor a fluttering nor an unfurling, but an undeniable *something*. There's something about these eyes distinctly different from all the kissers she's seen before. Something that makes the princess's breath catch.

"Hi," the girl mumbles.

(They're both girls again, somehow. Now that she's seen her eyes)

"Hi," the princess echoes before a cough at her left reminds her of herself. "Or… hello. Welcome. Thank you for waiting."

The girl looks away and nods slightly. The princess holds out her right hand expectedly, but instead of lips, rough, calloused fingers find her skin. The Last Princess of Rosenly fights to keep her expression frozen. She's always disliked it more when kissers take it upon themselves to reposition her for their own benefits. It's always felt more like a claiming, somehow. A tongue in her mouth is a necessity. Fingers on her skin are a choice.

And yet, the princess is still curious. Eager, almost, for the first time in years. Maybe this is the kind of thing a lover can be taught to unlearn.

The stranger's grip goes tight. She pulls at the princess's arm so suddenly that as she stumbles to her feet, she can't stop her shock from escaping through her lips. "What—"

The girl pins her against her chest and presses a knife to her throat.

"Don't. Move."

Sylvie

Sylvie Castell will never get any wishes, but if she had one, she'd wish for someone to actually listen to her for once.

(This is far from the truth, but Sylvie Castell will never get any wishes, so the truth is irrelevant)

But the princess moves.

Sylvie's prepared herself for that, of course. Sylvie Castell has never been an optimist. She might have acted like she'd thought the stars might answer under daylight to appease her constellation, but she's already prepared herself for the reality that they won't. She doesn't need to keep the princess in her grasp for longer than a few seconds, because she knows the ground is not about to open up and whisk them far away from the castle. If the princess runs, ducks, or attacks, it should barely change Sylvie's plans.

But she doesn't. Instead, nonsensically, the princess begins to giggle.

It starts so quietly that it takes Sylvie half a moment too long to process how violently her shoulders are shaking. By the time she's able to readjust the dagger well enough to accommodate the movement, she's already nicked her. She's expecting that to at least make her stop, but instead, the princess's laughter grows thicker and bolder. All at once, Sylvie's captive's body is folding in on itself. She can't move the knife quickly enough to stop it from digging further into her flesh.

It's unsettling. It's unnerving. Sylvie's prepared herself for dozens of different irrational reactions, but not for this.

And now, her weapon's on the ground and there's blood seeping into the grooves on her knuckles.

Sylvie attempts to keep her focus on the plan. This shouldn't change anything either.

(Except there's blood on her knife)

She never truly needed to hold onto the princess. She's threatened her. People saw. She's succeeded.

(Except there's blood on her fingers)

Even if the stars don't respond—perhaps especially if the stars don't respond—Sylvie's done what she set out to do. She's atoned.

(Except she's hurt someone)

She knows she should try to reclaim the weapon, but she can't trust her fingers to wrap around its handle, so instead, she lunges for the princess. Assassins don't stop at a bit of laughter, after all. If it doesn't look real, it'll all be for nothing.

Sylvie won't mess up again. She can't.

(She always does. She can never help herself)

No matter what happens next, she knows she'll be dragged to the dungeon after this. This is her one and only chance.

(She can never help herself)

She throws an arm around the princess's midsection and tugs her into her chest. She presses the other to her still-bleeding neck and takes one single, stumbling step away from the crowd.

"Don't come any closer!" she shrieks. "Stay back!"

The guards hesitate before moving and she feels her pulse begin to hammer. They need to apprehend her quickly. If she has too much time to think, she'll do something reckless.

(She can never help herself)

"I'm—I'll kill her," she tries, though she's holding no weapon. "I'll—"

Finally, she's tackled to the ground. An instinct she doesn't quite understand causes Sylvie to twist midair, inadvertently protecting the princess's body from impact instead of her own.

Sylvie hears shattering.

Sylvie hears shattering and she knows it's supposed to terrify her but it doesn't. Sylvie hears shattering and she knows it means she won't be coming back from this, but it's comforting, in a way. For once, her future is so incredibly clear that there's nothing she can do to destroy it further.

Sylvie Castell wasn't born to be a martyr, but most people aren't born for anything at all. At least this will be a meaningful thing to transform herself into.

The princess is helped up and swept into the waiting arms of her parents.

As guards drag Sylvie to her feet, she sees the fleeting confirmation of her own damnation. Splattered against the princess's back, already disappearing almost entirely into the air, is the twinkling of the starlight that was supposed to preserve Sylvie's sanity.

She finally allows her shoulders to relax. She doesn't bother looking toward the crowd, because she already knows there won't be anyone there looking back.

And so, with her head held high and her pulse the calmest it's felt in years, Sylvie allows herself to be escorted toward damnation.

Cell

The Last Princess of Rosenly

The last princess of Rosenly is supposed to be upset. She knows this. An attempt on her life is a terrible, dangerous thing.

It's also—though no one but her seems willing to admit it—an incredibly ridiculous one.

The last princess of Rosenly has been dying for seventeen years and ten months. If the would-be-assassin from the courtyard wanted to kill her, she's come far too late.

And so, the last princess of Rosenly isn't upset, she's judgmental. Of the girl whose eyes were *something* and whose blade was sharp enough to wound, yet whose mind was apparently so dull that it had never once occurred to her that if she wanted the princess dead, all she had to do was wait a few more weeks. Perhaps the girl isn't her true love after all. The last princess of Rosenly would like to think her soulmate would be at least a bit more practical.

As she's whisked away to her room hours earlier than usual, the last princess of Rosenly does her best to react appropriately. She knows she'll inevitably be told off for her laughter in the courtyard, but that just means she has to play her part even more perfectly than usual until then. If she can't quite manage upset, she can at least attempt fright. People always love frightened princesses, after all.

(It's what makes them so appealing to rescue)

She speeds up her breathing as thick bandages are applied to her wounded neck, allowing her eyes to water and unfocus. She adopts an air of disorientation that allows her to further retreat into the numb dissociation she normally enters as she's dressed down for the day. She lets a bit of water— only a bit, of course. She is still a princess—spill down her chin when she's offered it and ensures that the maid who

19

applied the thick salve to her blood-bitten lips feels her ragged breath as she works. By the time her parents are ready to see her, the last princess of Rosenly has done such an effective job pretending to be terrified that she finds her breathlessness impossible to shake.

When the last princess of Rosenly's parents burst into her room, they're clutching each other's arms. It takes little more than a look from her mother to make all the maids and medics flee. They'll be back tomorrow, of course—the princess suffered a few minor scratches in her scuffle with the assassin, and there's nothing worse than a princess with marred skin—but for now, the princess is almost alone.

When they reach her bed, the king and queen finally disentangle themselves from each other. They sit on either side of the princess. Neither makes any attempt to reach for her.

"The threat's been subdued," her father says. "She's in the dungeon."

The princess is full of questions, but now is not the time to ask any of them. Besides, the assassin had the good sense to attack her in the morning. If she can get through this next part quickly enough, she might actually have an afternoon to herself for once.

"She claims she was working alone," her father continues.

"Okay," the princess says. She wonders if he's implying exactly what she's been thinking about all morning. It would be ridiculous to attempt to kill the princess so close to her eighteenth birthday. Ridiculous, that is, unless it hadn't been a murder attempt at all.

Something's coming. The last princess of Rosenly knows it and she's almost certain her parents do too, but she also knows they won't want to know that she does. Her parents brought an entire kingdom together to wish for a child, once upon a time. Children are not meant to spend any amount of time contemplating their impending doom.

The last princess of Rosenly might never give them an heir, but she can at least offer them her naivety. She remains silent.

"People are... nervous," the queen contributes. "Angry on your behalf, of course, but also nervous."

"Of course."

"If we don't handle this discreetly, that could hurt attendance."

"Oh." The princess doesn't allow herself to smile at that. Parents who beg the skies for children don't deserve one who doesn't relish every opportunity to save herself.

"After your show this morning—"

The princess already knows it's coming, but she winces all the same. She made a mistake.

(She often does)

Half of Rosenly's already desperate for excuses to call her cursed or unnatural or inhuman, and when there was a blade at her throat, she laughed in their faces.

(Princesses are supposed to swoon)

(Princesses are supposed to cry)

The king puts a hand on his queen's knee and she falls silent. He reaches over the last princess of Rosenly to do it. His fingers never once brush against her lap. "She was scared," he feeds her.

"I was scared," the princess echoes.

"She was in shock."

"I was in shock."

The king nods once before turning to look at her. He never lets himself do that for too long at a time.

(It's difficult to face a child you know is temporary)

The princess averts her gaze so he doesn't have to.

"It would be wise to handle this quietly," he says. "We'll keep her for a while, see if she admits to anything, then hold off on the execution until…" the king trails off. The queen coughs. "Hopefully people will forget about her quickly. We'll keep her here until then. The prison's too public."

"Alright," the princess nods.

"It'd be best if none of us were seen anywhere near the dungeon in the meantime," her mother says. "She's a reckless young person looking for attention. No need to give it to her."

The princess frowns at that. "You won't be asking her—"

"We won't." The queen squeezes her king's fingers. She looks at the princess as she does. The last princess of Rosenly knows that must mean something. Her mother looks at her even more sparingly than her father does. "Understood?"

The princess's mouth's gone dry, but she still finds herself biting her cheek to keep from smiling. "Understood."

Her parents rise simultaneously, the conversation already finished. The last princess of Rosenly would normally just let them go, but today was not a normal day. She needs to know.

"Did the guards say anything?" she allows herself one single question. "About her eyes?"

Her mother slows. "Her eyes?"

"They were… different," she attempts to explain. "I think. I don't know how, but… they felt like they were."

She watches both her parents freeze. She's said too much. The last princess of Rosenly learned long ago that hope is an incredibly cruel thing to hand a parent.

"I don't believe so," her father finally says. "I'll have a guard inform you if any of them report otherwise."

"Thank you," she nods at his back.

She watches them leave. She runs her finger along the bandage at her neck.

Then, she pushes herself off the bed and sets off in search of a more appropriate outfit for the evening.

She has a failed assassin to go kiss.

Sylvie

Weavers can't sleep alone in Rosenly anymore.

The last time they safely could, Sylvie was too young and oblivious to notice how terrified that made everyone. All she knew was that suddenly, she went from being ushered out of her parents' bedroom every night to sleeping right beside them on the living room floor, her bed wedged between theirs and Bash's bassinet. As the stars continued to disappear she was dimly aware that it wasn't normal for the other families in their constellation to take turns sleeping at each other's homes, but all children yearned for sleepovers, so if anything, Sylvie was thrilled. No one wanted to tell her what was really happening.

The King and Queen of Rosenly—like all kings and queens—had wanted an heir. The King and Queen of Rosenly—like all kings and queens—had believed their bloodline so superior that its preservation was the kingdom's utmost priority.

Except the King and Queen of Rosenly couldn't conceive. So, when Sylvie had still been too young to even walk, they'd rounded up every weaver in the kingdom, amassed hundreds of wishers, and demanded the strings of fate be tangled, stretched, and mutilated until the stars gave them the daughter they craved. They'd ignored every warning about the fickleness of starlight, because the King and Queen of Rosenly—like all kings and queens—believed their child would become the most loved being in all the land. Finding a true love to anchor her to the ground should have been easy.

Then the princess passed eight, exhausted every eligible kissing candidate, and just as they'd promised they wouldn't, the King and Queen turned their vitriol upon the stars themselves. Starlight was cruel and cold, weaving was illegal, and one by one, the stars began to vanish. And Sylvie's constellation began to panic.

All living things need light, but weavers run on it. During the day they manage by sunlight, but there's supposedly no feeling better than lying beneath a star-speckled sky and drinking in its glow. Sylvie doesn't remember that, of course. She knows the glass roof of her childhood home was originally built to welcome in starlight, but in all but her fuzziest of memories, the sky above it is black and endless. Man-made light is supposedly less comfortable than starlight, but Sylvie can't remember the stars clearly enough to decide if sleeping by firelight really is that inferior. She does know it's more complicated, though. If a hearth goes out before the sun rises, a weaver's body reacts immediately: throwing them out of sleep with their heart in their throat and their fingers sometimes already too useless to relight the flame. So, they adapted. Bedrooms became obsolete. Constellations combined and expanded. Old rivalries and grudges were abandoned. For over a decade, the weavers of Rosenly have prioritized one thing and one thing only: making sure no weaver sleeps alone.

Sylvie rolls over on her cot. It's thin enough that she can feel the cool stone floor beneath it so she knows it'd be easy to move, but she doesn't let herself. There's a single window in the castle's small dungeon, and it's on the wall opposite her bars, just a few feet out of reach. Her cot's in the furthest possible corner from it. She's already been delivered her dinner, but she knows someone else might still be coming.

She will not give anyone the satisfaction of knowing how desperate she is to avoid the dark. As she watches the last remnants of daylight slip away she already knows she'll inevitably end up pressed against the bars trying to follow them, but she's going to preserve her dignity until the last possible moment.

The problem with martyrdom is there's often no one to comfort you through it. Sylvie's a realist. She's always known that redemption is inherently selfish; that's what makes true atonement impossible. But now, she's alone in the dark, mentally chanting to herself that she's done the right thing, with blood on her knuckles and no one to congratulate her for any of it. She's seconds away from insanity for a future she'll be too far gone to, see and all she wants to be is curled up beside a fireplace, letting someone else fix her mistakes.

And then, from the darkness, comes a clanging of metal. She jumps to her feet as the wall to the left of her cell creaks open to reveal a hidden door.

And then light. At last. Shaking and wavering and far too weak for Sylvie's liking, but light nonetheless.

"Hello." The princess nearly trips over herself as she stumbles through the doorway.

Sylvie sees why immediately. For some inconceivable reason, the princess has strapped herself into seemingly random bits and pieces of armour that were clearly never meant to be used together, none of which come remotely close to fitting her bony frame. A chainmail mask covers her face, eye-slits positioned so low that Sylvie would be surprised if the princess could see anything at all. The chest plate she's tied around herself could fit at least three of her, the sleeves beneath it hang far enough past her hands to pool in the meal tray she's holding, and her metal boots are so wide that Sylvie can't believe she made it through the door.

None of that matters, though. Because at the end of one of those sagging, chainmail sleeves, clutched in the princess's unarmoured hand, is a single, flickering torch.

26

Sylvie has to dig her nails into her palms to keep from leaping towards it. The princess doesn't need to know how desperately she wants to feel its light.

"I've come to deliver your dinner," the princess announces. It isn't until she does that Sylvie realizes she's adopted a tone so unbelievably low and gruff that it's nearly impossible to understand. The princess trips over her own feet again before adding, "I also wanted to say it was really brave. What you did back there. At the kissing line."

Now Sylvie's not just desperate, she's intrigued. "Yeah?"

"Yeah." Metal clangs as the princess attempts to nod. "Just... don't tell anyone I said that. Need to keep my job and all."

"Right, of course."

She doesn't know what the princess thinks she's doing, but if she has light with her, Sylvie's not about to complain. Or at least, she knows she shouldn't. But holding her tongue has never been a skill Sylvie's excelled at.

(She can never help herself)

The princess lights the lamp on the wall before putting out her torch against the stone floor. Finally, as light pours towards Sylvie, she begins to relax. And instantly becomes a bit too comfortable.

"I umm..." the princess returns to the bars. "Dinner. Here." She positions the tray at the meal slot and waits for Sylvie to accept it.

"I already got dinner," Sylvie challenges her instead. Because she was far from the right weaver for this mission, yet the others sent her anyway.

(Because maybe, they want her to fail)

(Because maybe, she's less dangerous in a dungeon)

"Right," the princess nods. "Of course. I just meant... dessert!" she decides. "This one's dessert."

"The Royal family serves their prisoners dessert?"

"Of course, we're not monsters." The princess either doesn't catch or chooses to ignore the malice in her tone. "They!" she quickly corrects herself. "Or I mean, they are. Obviously. Which is why we hate them. I bet they gave you all their least favourite foods just to spite you."

"Right." Sylvie gets up to grab the tray, then sits cross-legged on the stone floor to eat it. Broccoli and potatoes. Decidedly not dessert and exactly what she already ate a few hours ago. She doesn't let herself look at the princess as she picks up the fork. She can't let her know how curious she is about her next move. This might still be salvageable.

The princess half-sits, half-falls her way to the ground. Beyond the sound of Sylvie's fork against her plate, they're both silent.

The princess taps her fingers together. Sylvie does her best to not stare at them too obviously. The light beneath the princess's skin might be a cruel, unnatural version of starlight, but it's still starlight. It's the closest Sylvie's been to it in years.

And it's mesmerizing.

"I wanted to talk to you, I guess," the princess interrupts her not-staring. "To say how much I appreciate what you tried to do."

"Yeah?" Sylvie leans forward. "What did you like about it?"

"The umm... I want them dead. Obviously. All of the umm... they're *bad*."

Sylvie almost laughs. Clearly no one was ever planning on this princess living long enough to rule anything at all. She's far too terrible a liar to be Queen. "Must suck working for them then, huh? Bet they're all assholes."

"I... yes," the princess agrees. "Assholes."

Even with her ridiculous voice, it's incredibly obvious how uncomfortable the statement makes her. Potentially due to its crudeness, possibly due to its nature. Sylvie decides to try and push it.

(She's never met anything she didn't try to push)

"'specially the princess. Hear she's a real bitch."

"Of course," the princess nods diplomatically. "I agree."

"I heard," Sylvie drops her voice, leaning towards the bars. "She even makes her maids hold her toothbrush for her. She can do it on her own just fine, but she claims her wrists are 'too important to risk straining.'"

"I... yes," the princess clears her throat. "I've heard about that too. Quite annoying."

"And does she actually refuse to chew her own food too? Because she has to 'protect her mouth for kissing'?"

"Well, I suppose spending that much time on it might—"

"And does she actually refuse to wipe her own ass? Because even her hands are too pure to—"

"How long have you known?" The princess tugs off her mask, tossing it aside. To her credit, Sylvie genuinely hadn't considered she might be competent enough to realize she was making fun of her.

"Whaaaat?" She clutches a hand to her heart in mock horror. "Skies and stars, Your Highness!" She hastily scrambles to her feet to bow. "If I'd known it was you, I never would have—"

"Oh, shut up."

Sylvie does. If only because it was the last reaction she'd been expecting. Princesses could, apparently, occasionally grow spines.

And now that some of the armour's gone, Sylvie can see the bandage at her neck. She swallows. That hadn't been part of the plan. Sylvie suffers no illusions that kingdoms can be taken down without bloodshed, but that specific instance of it hadn't been needed.

She picks at her cuticles. Her cell has a single waste chute in the corner partitioned by a thin curtain, but other than that and her cot, it's entirely bare. She doesn't know if she'll ever have the opportunity to wash her hands.

By the time Sylvie's attention returns to the princess, she's already shed most of her armour and is in the process of crouching down to unfasten her too-large boots. The princess notices her staring.

"How long have you known?" she repeats. "I even changed my voice, so I—"

"Is that what you think guards sound like?" Sylvie realizes.

"Some of them do!"

She scoffs. Of course the princess has no idea what any of her staff sounds like. She's probably never even considered speaking to them. "Even if you hadn't done a truly terrible job there, anyone would've known," she admits. "You left your hands uncovered and you're kind of—" she gestures vaguely at her star-speckled fingers, latching onto a few of their threads to make the light speed up. "Recognizable."

The princess gasps, jumping back. She stares at her hands. "You just—how did you…" She tears off her chest plate and scrambles to escape the rest of her chainmail, exposing even more starlight.

Sylvie lets herself play with that too. It feels as though it's been a lifetime since she last got to touch starlight, but now, moving it is as simple as breathing.

"You're a weaver," the princess whispers.

"As if you didn't already know," the dungeon was set up to be lit and wasn't. The princess arrived with a torch just before she was plunged into complete darkness. Sylvie can recognize a threat when she sees one.

The princess just keeps staring at her arms. Sylvie makes the starlight spin faster. It feels good to finally be interacting with some again, even if it's trapped beneath the skin of a girl who will never come anywhere close to deserving any of it.

"Stop it!" the princess shrieks. At first, Sylvie attributes it to some kind of royal-bred need to be in control of everything at all times, but then when the princess starts clawing at her own skin, she realizes she's misread her. This isn't entitlement, it's fear.

And for Sylvie, that's a very, very positive development.

The Last Princess of Rosenly

The girl in the cell is *moving her skin*.

The last princess of Rosenly's parents couldn't have known she could do that. If they had, they would have warned her. They wouldn't have sent her down here all alone.

Except they hadn't truly sent her, had they? She'd just assumed. Read between the lines. Perhaps this time, they truly wanted her to stay away.

And now, they're going to find her dead on their dungeon floor and realize she was exactly as useless as everyone worried she was.

(She's never been smart enough to save herself)

She only had to survive two more months to not embarrass them further, and she couldn't even do that.

She needs to at least do that.

"Stop it!" she repeats, but the last princess of Rosenly already knows that strangers rarely stop when she wants them to. She digs her nails into her forearms. Maybe if she makes the first puncture herself, the rest of the starlight will escape through there. She won't be able to survive more than a few moments without it, but at least this way, she'll be in control. Creating one hole herself is better than allowing the prisoner to tear her apart.

(Princesses worthy of saving rarely get to stop anything at all)

The prisoner's standing right in front of the bars now, though the last princess of Rosenly can't recall her moving. All that matters—all that's ever mattered—is the light beneath her skin.

"Let me go." The prisoner makes the mistake of assuming that the last princess of Rosenly is the kind of princess who gets to bargain. "Sneak me off the castle grounds, then once we get far enough, I'll—"

"Stop!" The princess rolls onto her side. All the starlight's moving now. Each pinprick will tear through layer after layer of skin before fleeing to the sky two months too early, leaving her cold, empty corpse behind. Maybe they've already started to.

(Princesses worthy of saving rarely get to stop anything at all)

There's blood under her nails already, but that hasn't done anything to alleviate the pressure. She needs to work faster.

"If you just get me past the gate, I might still consider—"

"Stop it!"

She's going to die. The last princess of Rosenly's spent her entire life dying and she'd thought she'd accepted that, but suddenly, she can't. She's going to die and it's not until the moment it's actually happening that she finally realizes how desperately she wants to live.

"Unlock the cell!" The prisoner has to shout to be heard over her screaming. "Just… all you have to do is unlock the cell, alright? Then I'll—"

"Make it *stop!*" The princess tries to work faster, but her nails are too short. Dying's made them brittle.

(Princesses worthy of saving rarely get to stop anything at all)

She's pulling up skin, not starlight. She needs to get the stars *out*. "Stop it! Make them stop! Make—"

"I already did."

All at once, the prisoner's kneeling down across from her. The last princess of Rosenly can't remember when that happened either. "A while ago, actually. You're okay."

The princess blinks. Slowly, she allows herself to look at her arms. They're covered in red and white scratches and her fingertips are sticky with blood, but the starlight's normal. Not completely still—it's never completely still—but normal. And it's *still there*.

"No," she mutters, starting to scratch again. "No, you didn't—they're still—make them stop! Get it out! Make—"

(Princesses worthy of saving rarely get to stop anything at all)

"Hey!" The prisoner tries to shove her arm through the bars, but the princess is quicker.

She darts away, pressing herself against the wall. "Get them out! We need to—"

"You need to calm down! You—"

"They need to stop! I can't let them—"

"You're—"

"Why won't they—"

"Stars, Estrella!"

The last princess of Rosenly freezes. She hasn't heard that name in a very, very long time.

"That's your name, isn't it?" The prisoner's voice is quieter now, almost gentle. Her eyes aren't, though. They're dark and desperate. Wide and wild. "Wasn't that what—"

"No one's supposed to call me that," she stops her.

(Princesses worthy of saving rarely get to stop anything at all)

"Okay," the prisoner nods. The princess hates how much her voice has already changed. For once, the last princess of Rosenly had felt like the kind of princess worth threatening. People always love frightened princesses, though.

(It's what makes them so appealing to rescue)

34

"Alright," the prisoner's still nodding. Still speaking to her as if she's made of glass instead of starlight. "What do I call you, then?"

She doesn't respond. She hugs her chest. She picks at her skin.

"Estrella."

The last princess of Rosenly's head snaps up. She glares. "I said you're not supposed to—"

"My name," the prisoner slowly raises both arms into the air, palms open and facing the princess. "Is Sylvie. Sylvya, actually, but I don't like that one all that much either. If you wanted to get name-hate revenge, or something."

"The stars," she suddenly remembers. "I need to—"

"Estrella," the prisoner interrupts. "Tell me who I am."

"Sylvya," she brushes her off. She needs to get back to work. "I have to—"

"Of course you caught that part," the prisoner's still speaking. "Close enough, I guess. Tell me where we are."

"I… dungeon. But the stars—"

"Right. We're in your dungeon. Who can hurt you here?"

If she could just get the starlight out, then—

"Estrella!"

"That's not my name!" she erupts. "No one's supposed to call me that! You can't—"

"Okay," the prisoner's voice is unbelievably soft. "Tell me the right one later then, okay? Who can hurt you here?"

Her eyes narrow. Her focus collapses in on the prisoner in the cell. "You," she whispers.

The prisoner shakes her head. "No, not me. I'm stuck all the way over here, remember? You're the only one who can do anything to you right now."

"But the stars—"

"Are just light," the prisoner says. "They're just light. And I'm the expert, okay? So you have to trust me."

"You tried to kill me!"

"I did. And if I could've done that by just spinning a few stars, neither of us would be here right now, right?"

The princess blinks. Tries to shake some sense into her head.

"I was just playing with the light, Princess," the prisoner says softly. "You shouldn't have even been able to feel anything. Did you? I didn't think—"

The princess hesitates, considering. She can't remember. She knows she must have felt something since she reacted so strongly, but now, she can't remember what. "You tried to kill me!" she clings to.

"And I failed. And I'm not trying to right now. You need to breathe, Princess. Why would I waste this much time trying to calm you down if I was planning on hurting you. Slowly, the comment pushes its way to whatever part of the princess's brain is still behaving rationally. She draws a long breath, finally letting herself slump against her spine. She's abruptly exhausted. She's abruptly extremely aware of how much blood's clinging to her fingertips.

(There's nothing worse than a princess with marred skin)

The prisoner—*Sylvie*—clears her throat. "You umm... first time meeting a weaver, I take it?"

"Shut up," she hisses.

The prisoner nods, but keeps talking anyway. "I can fix that, you know. Your arms. Before you do… whatever it is you came here to do."

The princess stares at her.

"I mean, if you're gonna keep looking at a few scratches as if they're the end of the world, I might as well—"

"Why would I trust you to do that?"

"Because I'm in a cell," she shrugs. "And I don't know why you're here, but it's clearly not to let me go, which means I kind of have a vested interest in you not going back up those stairs looking like someone attacked you."

The princess doesn't respond. She's already trying to puzzle out how to explain any of this. Her body's her most important asset, after all. She doesn't know if her parents will be angrier if they find out she damaged it herself, or if she lies and says she gave a prisoner the opportunity to. This is the first time she's been allowed to visit one alone. If they find out anything went wrong, it will be the last time she's ever allowed to do anything alone at all.

"Please," the prisoner's voice trembles slightly. It pulls the princess back out of her head.

Would-be-assassins don't have voices that tremble. They certainly don't say please.

"I'm a weaver who hasn't gotten the chance to grant a wish in decades, Princess," the prisoner whispers. "I couldn't even get an assassination attempt right. Just… please let me fix something for once, okay?"

The princess swallows. Chews a flap of skin off her lip. There really is only one option.

(There's nothing worse than a princess with marred skin)

"What would I need to do?"

Sylvie

"Give me your hands."

Sylvie has absolutely no idea if wishes even work when the stars you're calling upon aren't in the sky, but she isn't about to pass up the opportunity to try. Besides, these stars are physically contained to the princess's skin. If they can do anything, it should be healing her.

(And Sylvie desperately wants an excuse to touch them)

(And Sylvie desperately needs to fix something)

The princess doesn't move.

"It won't work as well if we're not touching, Princess."

"It's just…" The princess chews at her swollen, already-bloodied lips. Sylvie does her best to conceal her revulsion. "Will it hurt?"

"No," she thinks.

Slowly, the princess approaches the bars. "I control it." She wraps her fingers over Sylvie's instead of intertwining them.

Sylvie feels her shoulders loosen as starlight presses against her skin. The other weavers were right. This is infinitely better than any manmade flame. "Alright," she manages. "That's fair. You need to tell me the wish. Speak it first, then think it while I repeat it. It should be brief, but specific. Can't have you going back upstairs with an already healed neck."

"This is illegal," the princess whispers.

"Yeah." She's supposed to be being gentle, but that's a hard façade to uphold in the face of so much ignorance.

(She can never help herself)

"Not like your family aren't experts at picking and choosing which laws to follow, though. I won't tell anyone if you don't."

The princess considers. "What if you're the one who—"

"Weavers can't make wishes." She needs the conversation to be done with before she destroys it further. Now that she's this close to starlight, she's desperate to weave it. "It upsets the balance."

"But aren't I... like you?"

Sylvie recoils before she can stop herself. "You are *nothing* like me. I'm a weaver, not an abomin—"

The princess pulls away.

She winces. "Sorry. That wasn't personal."

Her cheek twitches. "Kinda felt like it."

Sylvie doesn't know why she insists on hurling herself towards disaster

(she can never help herself)

but now, she needs to remain calm. Maybe if she does, she might even leave the princess feeling so indebted to her that she won't put the light out when she goes. Or do whatever it is she came to the dungeon to do. Because now, Sylvie doesn't want to be a martyr or a revolutionary or a sacrifice, she just wants to be okay.

She takes a deep breath. "Sorry," she forces herself to repeat. "Take my hands again, alright? Let me help."

The princess cocks her head to the side. It makes the veins along her neck more pronounced. "You apologize too much for an assassin."

"Yeah, well you consort with criminals too much for a princess."

Star-speckled fingers wrap around hers before Sylvie can even think about taking it back. "What do I say?"

She readjusts her grip. "I wish all the wounds I've given myself today would heal themselves."

She waits for the princess to echo her.

"Now think it," Sylvie instructs. "Think that and only that. Those exact words. And mean it."

The princess nods, her lips moving to silently repeat the phrase. It takes a moment, but eventually, Sylvie sees it. Thin strings of sparkling gold spread from their joined fingers into the waiting air. The threads never become too long—it isn't a particularly strong wish, after all—but that hardly matters. The princess's starlight's already there waiting. Sylvie waits for the light to imprint itself upon her eyelids before letting them fall shut.

Sylvie hasn't seen anyone weave in almost a decade,

(This is also a lie, but one she needs to tell herself is true)

but that hardly matters. A weaver's connection to the stars isn't something that's taught, it's something that just is. She traces each tendril along her eyelids, imagining them descending and locking themselves with the starlight beneath the princess's skin. It's the opposite direction she'd normally pull it in and far from a traditional anchoring, but it's still stars. They're still light. She knows it'll work the moment the threads allow themselves to be woven together, but her confidence is confirmed when she hears the princess gasp. She opens her eyes just in time to watch the remnants of the princess's quickly-closing scratches seal themselves. It's mesmerizing. And something Sylvie can never admit she's already itching to do again. She longs to keep her fingers wrapped around the light for as long as possible, but the princess is already staring at her skin in awe, so she knows if she holds on for too long, she'll quickly realize Sylvie's just as captivated.

So, she pulls away. She takes a step back. The princess came undone at a few swirling specks of light. Sylvie's surprised she's still standing at all after seeing actual weaving.

"I didn't realize they'd move like that," she mumbles. "Probably should have warned you." It's not an apology. She can't offer those anymore, now that the princess's noticed.

"And I'm probably supposed to thank you." The princess meets her eye and holds it in the silence that follows. It's not a thank you either. Sylvie's almost impressed.

Now, though, comes the difficult part.

"What happens now?" Sylvie accidentally whispers. "Why are… if you want revenge, you've already got it. I'm trapped in a cell."

"You think I'm here for revenge?"

"I tried to kill you an hour ago then you snuck into the dungeon in disguise. Kinda the most natural conclusion to jump to there."

The princess chews on her lip whenever she's thinking. Sylvie already hates it. People who've gotten everything shouldn't get to destroy themselves so willingly. "You're… nice," she eventually says. "For an assassin."

"I am not!"

"You helped me, though," the princess pushes. "When I was scared. You—"

"Maybe I just don't enjoy listening to nonsensical screaming!"

"What's wrong with your hands?"

Sylvie blinks against the tonal change. "What?" She surveys them before rolling her eyes. "It's not my blood, Princess. You were there."

"They're scratched up too, though."

Sylvie already knows that. She's spent the past few

41

hours attempting to pick the blood off. But her scratches are surface level. They require no treatment and warrant no mentioning. "That's not… why are you here, Princess?"

"Because I was hoping you'd be interesting," she shrugs, plopping onto the stone floor. "I'm not going to kill you, Sylvie. Corpses are much less entertaining."

She seizes her chance. "You should leave the light going when you go then. I might be interesting twice."

The princess frowns. As she shifts her neck again, thin, dark hair falls over her shoulder. Then, she almost begins to smile. "Are you… afraid of the dark?"

Sylvie scoffs. "Thought we'd already established I'm a weaver."

"What does that have to do with anything?"

She doesn't respond. Instead, she crosses her arms over her chest and turns her attention to the floor. She won't be made to lay out her every weakness to someone who clearly already knows them.

She hears the princess stand and panics. She's pushed things a little too far.

(She can never help herself)

"What are—"

"Sounds like we'll be needing more oil, then," the princess says. "I'll go fetch some. On one condition, though."

Sylvie fights to keep her expression neutral. She should refuse. She should let the princess leave and take the light with her. The longer she's able to function, the more opportunities she'll have to ruin everything.

(She can never help herself)

But she's scared and desperate and was never the right weaver for this mission, so she already knows she'll agree to anything to save herself from the darkness.

"What?" Sylvie says.

The princess smiles. It's haunting, through her
cracked, bleeding lips. "I get to stay as long as the light does."

The Last Princess of Rosenly

The last princess of Rosenly will never rule anything at all.

Though she's been the technical sole heir to the throne since birth, her only true inheritance has always been her impending doom. She was not raised on politics or battle strategy; she was rarely even afforded control over her own attire.

But now, she has a girl in a dungeon. And for the first time, there's no one telling her how to handle that but herself.

She practically skips her way back through the tunnels.

Being so palpably thrilled by the prospect of having a captive listener might not make the last princess of Rosenly a particularly good person, but she's never needed to be good anyhow. She was pretty, once. She's tragically beautiful, now. Goodness does not do nearly as much for dying princesses.

She can feel the prisoner—*Sylvie*—watching her as she refills the lamp, but the princess keeps her back turned. Her initial entry into the dungeon was rushed and clumsy. This time, she won't speak until the prisoner does. This time, she's going to make it abundantly clear that she's the one in charge. It's not an ideal way to begin a courtship, but it's the least terrifying one at her disposal.

"That's it, then?" The prisoner eventually gives up on her brooding. She doesn't mention the bucket in the princess's fist, though. Though her eyes haven't left it since she brought it into the dungeon. "You're just gonna sit there creepily watching me all night?"

The last princess of Rosenly shrugs. "I haven't got anything better to do."

"Why are you really here, Princess? I'm too quiet for entertainment."

She chews at her lip, considering her answer. The last princess of Rosenly is nowhere near as stupid as she pretends to be. Whether she was planning on going through with it or not, the prisoner tried to kill her a few hours ago. She's under no illusion that they'll instantly jump to love declarations or even a mutual acceptance of each other's existences, nor does she want to. But she also knows that the prisoner's hands shook when she pulled her against her chest. That her eyes were even more frantic than the princess had felt while she'd been attempting to tear herself to shreds on the dungeon floor. That she carefully avoids looking at the bandage on the princess's neck, her fingers keep picking at the blood on her skin, and her gaze keeps darting toward the bucket.

The prisoner is not going to deliver any true love's kisses tonight and she's far from the first person The Last Princess of Rosenly would have chosen, but she might be the only one left. And for the first time in a decade, the princess gets to control when and how they test it.

"Assassination attempts are typically punishable by death," she eventually says. "After a thorough investigation, of course."

The prisoner doesn't seem intimidated by that in the slightest. It feeds the princess's theory. The dagger was far from the last step in her plan. She lets it go though, for now. She'll press more once she's won herself more trust.

"Was that really your first time in the line?" she asks instead. "You seem younger. You should have—"

"Maybe I wasn't too eager to try and save the person punishing my people for the very thing she begged—"

"My parents begged," she corrects. "And punished. I just—"

"Same—"

"Do you want me to put out the light and leave?" she stops her.

The prisoner tries to glare at her, but she catches the brief flash where her eyes widen.

The princess sighs. "That wasn't a threat," she says. "But it seems you believe it would've been, if I was my parents. You don't get to keep blaming me for mistakes someone else made."

"Or what?" The prisoner crosses her arms. "If that wasn't a threat."

"I don't…" the last princess of Rosenly pinches her brow, reevaluating. She's not going to get the prisoner to tolerate her tonight. She might as well spend it doing something useful instead.

She marches the bucket over to the edge of the cell and sits on the floor beside it. "Give me your hands." She holds out a palm.

Instead, the prisoner takes a step back.

"You're ridiculously squeamish, you know. For an assassin." The last princess of Rosenly is not the one in a cell. This is *her* castle. She won't force the prisoner to pretend to like her, but she also won't allow herself to be continuously insulted. She deserves control.

(Princesses worthy of saving rarely get to control anything at all)

"I don't know what you're—"

"I was going to offer you a washcloth," the princess explains, pulling it from her pocket. "Since you're clearly so bothered by the blood. If you asked for it. I thought it'd be a show of good faith. But clearly good faith doesn't work on you, so we're doing this instead." She shakes her wrist. "Give me your hands."

"If you toss me the cloth, I can—"

"No," she stops her. "This is my dungeon. You are my prisoner. Any help or good grace you get is going to come from me and only me, so you can either waste away in the dark picking at your hands, or you can give in, admit you belong to me, and ask for help."

The prisoner snarls. "I don't belong to—"

"I'll go." The princess draws herself to her feet. She's in no rush. She's not the one who should be panicking. "After I put out the light, of course. I don't see why I'd keep it burning if you won't even tell me why you need it."

"You said I was nice," the prisoner reminds her.

The last princess of Rosenly shrugs, approaching the lamp. "You tried to kill me. For most people, that'd render all niceness irrelevant."

The prisoner just glares until her hand's already on the dial.

"Wait!" she breaks.

The princess does. She bites her lip to keep from grinning too obviously in triumph.

"You can't..." the prisoner starts. "It's like..." she sighs. "I need it, okay? Can't that be enough?"

"No." If she allows the prisoner to sit in stubborn silence, they'll never get anywhere.

And, she wants to know.

(Princesses worthy of saving rarely get to know anything at all)

The prisoner glares for a moment longer before looking away. She takes a deep breath. "It's... bad," she says. "It's... weavers don't last long in the dark."

"What does that mean?"

"You know!"

The princess stumbles back. She's doing this all wrong. She was attempting to elicit acceptance, not anger.

"That's why you lock up your weavers!" the prisoner continues. "You keep them in the dark long enough to destroy them, then you get to let them go and act like—"

"We let weavers go because we've used the stars too," she recites. "It wouldn't be just to punish anyone indefinitely for crimes we've also committed."

The prisoner practically growls. "Is that what they tell you? Is that what you hide behind so you can keep pretending you're anything less than a monster? It's torture," she spits. "You know it's torture, but as long as you don't have to physically touch someone to do it you get to keep pretending you're..." she trails off as the princess lowers her arm. "What are you..."

"Okay," she whispers. "I'll leave it on."

The prisoner frowns. "I thought you said... I just called you a monster."

"And I think you think you were being honest," she says. "I don't... I wanted answers, Sylvie. I won't tolerate being unjustly attacked for every little thing I do, but I don't want you lying about things to appease me either. I demanded an answer. You gave a real one. The light stays on."

She waits a beat for the prisoner to thank her.

She doesn't.

She returns to the bucket. "Now ask me to wash your hands."

"What if I don't?"

"Then you don't," the last princess of Rosenly shrugs. "I'm not going to beg you to help yourself."

"I can clean them myself."

She shakes her head. "I'm not going to let you do that either. I'm in charge here. The quicker you accept that, the easier this goes."

The prisoner just glares.

"Last time I'm offering, Sylvie."

She rolls her eyes. "Okay, fine." She sticks her fists through the bars. "Here."

"Ask."

"I'm not—"

"*Ask.*"

She sighs. "Just… get rid of it, alright?"

The last princess of Rosenly considers pushing for a 'please', but decides against it. Getting the prisoner to ask at all already feels like a triumph. Instead, she smiles. "Of course." She dips the cloth into the soapy water and presses it against the back of the prisoner's hand.

She hisses instantly.

The last princess of Rosenly laughs. "You're really sensitive, you know. For a—"

"If you're about to say for an assassin again, I'll kick that bucket over."

"That's not—"

Her eyes dart up to the princess's. "Thought you said you wanted honesty."

She did. She does. She smiles. "For an assassin."

The prisoner doesn't kick the bucket over. Her leg doesn't fit through the bars. The princess finds a bit too much joy in her desperate attempts to hop around on one foot until the pain dissipates.

"No one would be comfortable with old blood all over them," the prisoner mutters as she continues to scrub. "That doesn't make me squeamish. Or mean I regret anything."

"I never said I thought you did."

"Well, I'm just saying, most people—"

She stares pointedly at her own arms. The wish might have closed her cuts, but it didn't get rid of the blood.

"You don't count," the prisoner says. "You're…"

49

"An abomination?" she guesses.

"Yes. And seriously fucked in the head. You laugh when people try to kill you."

"Only when they're really bad at it."

"That's—"

"Done," the princess interrupts. "Switch hands." As she starts working on the other, she risks looking up. "Did you umm… speaking of that. This morning. When we first saw each other, did you feel any—"

She feels the prisoner go rigid. "You came here to kiss me," she realizes.

The princess blushes at that. She hates that she can physically feel herself losing control.

(Princesses worthy of saving rarely get to stop anything at all)

"You thought you'd what?" The prisoner steps away. "Sneak in a quick kiss before your parents kill me and parade my body through town like some kind of fucking symbol? You thought—"

"I mean, if you are my true love, I think they'd at least skip the parade."

The prisoner gapes. "That's… are you trying to make a joke right now?"

"Yes," she nods proudly.

"About my impending death?"

"Oh." The princess is so used to thinking about hers that she occasionally forgets it isn't a topic of casual conversation for most people. "Well," she recovers. "I at least thought it was funny."

The prisoner only glares at that.

"And I kiss all the prisoners," she explains. "Especially the ones dangerous enough to warrant execution. We can't risk anyone taking my salvation to the grave with them. I was just checking to see if you'd felt anything so we could speed this all up. You're not special."

"You came here to kiss me *because* I tried to kill you?" the prisoner reiterates.

"Yes."

"That's so fucked."

"Extremely. Which is why I thought it'd be more fun to pretend to be someone else entirely this time, but it wasn't... it was perhaps not the most well thought-out plan," she admits. "My parents come, normally. It's quick and formal and sometimes done at sword point. You're the first one they've decided it would be too risky to chance being seen bringing me to themselves."

"I'm flattered."

"You should be." She watches the prisoner carefully. "Because I don't want... I'm tired of being kissed like it's a favour. Or an obligation. So I'm not... you're going to want it. I'm not going to even consider kissing you until you want it, and then you're going to *beg*. I'll come back every night until—"

"I miraculously fall in love with you?"

"Or until you decide to get it over with and kiss me just to get me to leave you alone," the last princess of Rosenly says. "I don't particularly care. I just need you to know you're the one who asked for it."

"That's not going to happen."

"Alright," she shrugs. "Then I'll die in two months. Maybe you'll go first, but my parents are usually slow with these things. They probably won't want an execution interrupting our schedule. I can be civil if you can be civil, but if not, it'll just be a long two months. And if I go first," she glances pointedly towards the lamp. "It sounds like they might not have to worry about killing you after all." She nods

51

at the prisoner's hand. She's already started picking at it again. "Still need help with that one?"

She offers her palm back up.

"What if…" the prisoner quietly begins as she scrubs. "You thought you felt something, didn't you? When we first saw each other? That's why you asked?"

She doesn't respond. She bites her lip. She's given away too much.

"What if… if I had felt something," the prisoner continues. "When our eyes met. Possibly. You really think that might mean…"

The last princess of Rosenly has had years of etiquette lessons, but even she can't stop herself from grinning. "I guess you're stuck with me until we find out."

Sylvie

The princess is annoyingly committed to pretending to be civil.

Sylvie doesn't want that. She can't want it. She's supposed to be halfway to insanity already. If her bottled starlight hadn't broken in the courtyard, she would have poured it out herself.

(She wouldn't have been able to, but it's a comforting lie in retrospect)

A Sylvie who can think is a Sylvie who can decide, and a Sylvie who can decide will always be a Sylvie who decides wrong.

(She can never help herself)

It'd be safer for everyone else if she just gave up.

(Maybe that's why she's really here)

(Maybe they're not coming at all)

But Sylvie Castell will always decide wrong, so she asked the princess to keep the lamp burning her first night in the dungeon. And Sylvie Castell has always been selfish, so instead of lashing out at her enough to get her to change her mind the next night, she remains quiet and docile.

And the princess brings pie.

"Figured I owe you actual dessert," she says, but then she refuses to slide it through the meal slot until Sylvie asks for it, so she doesn't. It's an easy form of rebellion, after all. Sylvie's never been the kind of person who gets to just ask for things.

On the third night, the princess tosses her a small burlap sack.

"It's a puzzle," she explains. "I figured it probably gets boring down here."

It's a manipulation tactic. She's supposed to point out how dark it is in her cell and ask for more light to solve it by. Sylvie doesn't. Instead, she refuses to even open the bag. It feels too much like submission.

In the middle of her sixth day of imprisonment, Sylvie grows too bored to worry about her ego. There's more than one way to lose your mind, after all. Still, she promises herself she'll only work on it while she's alone. She won't give the princess the satisfaction of watching her struggle.

When the princess returns that night and finds the puzzle started, she smiles. It makes Sylvie want to slap her.

"I could bring you more," she offers softly. "If you're worried about finishing that one too quickly. Or something else, if you want. I'd offer books, but I figured—"

"I know how to read," Sylvie spits. "A crown isn't a prerequisite to literacy."

The princess's eyes narrow. "I was going to say," she says slowly. "That I wasn't sure it was bright enough in there for that. I can barely read out here as is, and I'm right below the lamp."

She scoffs. "Sure you were."

The princess frowns, moving closer to the bars. Sylvie hates it. There's starlight beneath her skin and she's a *person* and Sylvie's *alone*. She hates how excited the tiny action makes her.

"I don't understand why you're so determined to hate me, Sylvie."

She rolls her eyes. "What, not used to—"

"A lot of people don't like me," the princess stops her. "I know that. A crown isn't synonymous with stupidity either, but—"

"Could've fooled me."

"*Sylvie.*"

She licks her lips. She really shouldn't have given her her name. She doesn't know what she was thinking.

(She does, but she's not ready to confront that yet either)

"I'm the reason the stars are gone," the princess continues. "I get that. But I'm not... they'll be back. The moment I die or find my true love, my parents already promised they'd—"

"Your parents have already proven their word means nothing."

"And I'm not them!"

Sylvie bites her lip to keep herself from smiling. Comparisons to her parents are the quickest way to get under the princess's skin, and right now, she could do with a bit of excitement.

The princess sighs, pinching her brow. "I know you're lonely, Sylvie. You must be. It's been days. I'm... not saying it's the same, but I get that, okay? More than you know. I figured by now you'd at least—"

"Turn into some perfect, submissive soulmate just because you've given me a few things I didn't even want?" Maybe she'll be strong enough to do it this time. Maybe she'll push the princess far enough to give up on her altogether.

"No!" the princess exclaims. "That's not..." she takes a deep breath. "Alright, what do you, then?" she asks. "Want?"

"You to leave me alone." She doesn't. She can't bring herself to want it. She's too much of a coward.

"You don't mean that," the princess calls her bluff. "That's—I keep the lamp lit. And you..." she sighs. "I know you might think you do, but I know a thing or two about being lonely, Sylvie. Even if you can't like me, I know you still—"

She's gotten a bit too close to the truth, so Sylvie snaps. "Stars, Princess! Just fucking go!"

The princess watches her for a long moment, almost daring her to take it back. Sylvie doesn't. For better or worse, she's always been exceptional at not taking things back.

(She can never help herself)

Besides, she knows she doesn't have to worry. The princess showed her hand too early and now, threats of darkness no longer work. She'll be back tomorrow evening to relight the lantern. She's too desperate to see herself as a good person to risk it. As long as Sylvie doesn't kiss her, she'll be safe. Maybe even safe long enough to be rescued. It's all the safety of knowing she'll never be left in the dark, wrapped up in the comfort of being able to tell herself she at least tried to be. It's much easier to play a martyr when you don't truly need to mean it.

The princess pushes herself to her feet and silently leaves.

She doesn't put out the light as she goes, though. Because Sylvie was right.

Sylvie

Sylvie was wrong.

She tries to find triumph in the emptiness that fills the dungeon in the princess's absence, but it never comes. She's all alone. She has been for days. The princess gave up on everything but idle small talk days ago, so her not staying the night shouldn't change much.

But before, at least Sylvie hadn't been alone on her own. The guards who bring her meals are masked and silent. The princess wasn't. Sylvie hadn't realized how much she'd been relying on interacting with someone with a face.

The princess will be back tomorrow night, though. Probably even sooner. She's insufferably consistent. Sylvie pretends she's not watching the slightly discoloured crack in the wall where she now knows a door's hidden and does her best to at least come up with something snarky to say when the princess inevitably returns prematurely.

But she doesn't.

By the time Sylvie falls asleep, she's genuinely considering making herself a bit gentler, just to avoid being left alone again. Gentleness is dangerous, though. Gentleness might condemn them all. She's supposed to be resigning herself to the darkness.

By the time her lunch is delivered the next day, isolation's eaten away so much of her sanity that she briefly even considers apologizing.

When the sun starts to descend, Sylvie's disgusted to find herself welcoming it for all the wrong reasons. Darkness approaching means the princess will be here soon. Darkness is the only time she doesn't have to be alone.

But then, the princess doesn't come.

This time, Sylvie really does press herself against the bars as the light fades. A week can wear away a lot of self-worth.

(There's more than one way to go insane, after all)

She tells herself the princess must be timing things to arrive exactly as total darkness does and she knows it'll be mortifying to be found like this, but right now, none of that matters. All she cares about is holding onto the light for as long as possible.

Darkness, it turns out, feels a lot like drowning. Sylvie wasn't expecting that. She'd assumed that the instant the light disappeared, her body would shut down. Instead, it leaves and for a moment, she's just sitting in the chill of the first true darkness she's ever known.

It's a little serene. Almost calm.

And then her chest starts to scream.

Sylvie gasps for air and inhales far too much of it to house comfortably in her lungs, but it doesn't help. She knows air isn't the thing she's starving for, but she keeps gasping anyway.

(She can never help herself)

Sylvie lied. Her constellation knew the stars were unlikely to answer them in the courtyard beneath the light of day. They knew whoever they sent would likely end up here, doing exactly this.

And Sylvie knew that someone had to be her. It was the right decision. The *only* decision. Sylvie Castell had caused a lot of pain; it was high time she inflict some of it upon herself.

So, she lied. She said she'd sat in the dark before. Never for too long, of course—no one wants a reckless agent—but that she had. It was an easy lie, too. Sylvie was the kind of weaver who often went unaccounted for even within her own constellation, so of course no one would be able to verify whether or not she spent the occasional night alone.

She was just broken enough for her entire constellation to meet her claims with not surprise nor rebuttal, but quiet, almost understanding pity. So, she kept lying. In the days leading up to the assassination attempt, she really did start to sleep alone. She told the others she was practicing. Part of her had meant to practice.

But she couldn't. She'd never once been strong enough to face the dark. She'd been stupid enough to believe it might never actually come to this.

And then, once she'd accepted that it would, she'd been handed a princess so full of misplaced hope that she'd practically promised to keep the darkness away, and Sylvie was too stubborn to let her.

(She can never help herself)

She isn't going to die. Even as she wheezes and aches and drags herself over to her tiny cot, some part of her brain still knows she isn't going to die. But she's seen what darkness does firsthand; she knows that this will be worse.

"Shit." The speaker's practically shouting, but Sylvie can barely hear it over the roaring in her ears. "Shit, shit, shit, I—sorry, I—Stars, Sylvie! One moment, okay? Just give me—"

Sylvie squeezes her eyes shut against the shrill sound of metal scraping metal. For a moment, she hopes it's her bones grinding themselves to dust. At least then she wouldn't have to feel anymore.

And then, there's a hand on her shoulder.

She swipes at it instinctively.

The princess jumps back. Her eyes look just as panicked and wild in the torchlight as Sylvie's pulse feels. Hesitantly, she steps within range and crouches down to attempt to meet her gaze. Sylvie doesn't let her. "Does this… does it help? With the torch being closer? You didn't say much about it—or I guess you don't say much about anything at all, actually, unless it's to yell at me about something trivial, but—" The princess always gestures far too much while talking. Normally Sylvie brushes it off as just another of her mildly annoying traits, but now, it's all she can focus on.

She catches her wrist. The princess flinches, but she doesn't attempt to break free. She could right now, and Sylvie knows it. Darkness has made her too weak to even curl her fingers properly.

Sylvie pulls the princess's hand closer. She stares at the light dancing across her skin. Then, she presses the princess's fingers to her pounding forehead and slowly breathes into her palm.

Eventually, impossibly, Sylvie begins to relax. With that comes a vulnerability that makes her deeply uncomfortable. Her shoulders slump. Her eyes fall shut. She doesn't have enough energy left to be anything but docile.

Sylvie decides to give herself exactly ten seconds to pull her mind back together before she pushes the princess away again.

Then, she takes over a minute.

And forgets how to push.

Instead, as Sylvie slowly releases the princess's wrist, she simply says, "You brought a weapon into my cell."

"I did," the princess says. "You were screaming."

"I was?"

She nods. "I couldn't hear it until I opened the door. The dungeon's…" she grimaces, faint traces of colour giving temporary life to her sunken cheeks. "I guess I never really considered why the dungeon's soundproof. Or I did and just didn't want to know. I should've asked. I'm sorry."

Sylvie doesn't know what to do with that, so instead, she sits up straighter and pulls each of her limbs as far from the princess as possible. "Didn't think you'd actually see that through," she admits. "Just my luck the one time a royal decides to keep their word, it's when they're threatening me."

The princess's eyes widen. "That's not—I didn't mean to be late. This had nothing to do with yesterday, it was just... bad timing."

"Sure, Princess."

"That's not my name."

Sylvie almost smiles at that. She's not sure why. "Give me one, then."

The princess doesn't respond. She blows out the already dying torch and for a moment Sylvie's breath leaps, but she's safe. She knows she's safe. The lamp on the wall's burning just as brightly as any other night. Tonight, she just might have to remind herself of that a bit more frequently.

She's expecting the princess to relock the cell and curl up under the lamp with yet another book, but instead, she tosses the torch aside, puts her book and blankets against their usual wall, and reenters the cell.

Sylvie stares.

"Don't bother trying to run. There's a guard right on the other side of the tunnel," the princess lies. "It's why they keep letting me down here."

"What are—"

"I just came into your cell with a weapon," she reminds her. "If you're still trying to assassinate me, you're clearly terrible at it. If I'm stuck wasting all my time down here, we might as well make some progress on that fucking puzzle."

The Last Princess of Rosenly

"Part of me thought you were lying, you know."

The prisoner doesn't move to help with the puzzle, but the last princess of Rosenly already saw that coming. She's clearly not the kind of person who helps with anything at all.

(Unless the princess is hurt)

(Unless the princess is terrified)

"A big part of me, actually," she admits. "About the dark? I thought you might've been too embarrassed to admit you were just afraid of it."

"Sounds like you don't know anything about your own people," the prisoner snarls. She's retreated to her cot, leaning against the wall to watch the princess scrutinize puzzle pieces beneath the flickering lamp light. Her shoulders are still shaking slightly, but the princess knows better than to point that out.

"Sounds like it," she agrees. "I didn't mean to... I won't be late again, alright? I promise."

The prisoner scoffs. "How late were you?"

"Five minutes, give or take."

The prisoner draws a sharp, audible breath.

"Sylvie?" she checks. "Are you—"

"Puzzle's harder than you thought, huh?"

She lets her change the topic. "It's dark," she says. "You've had multiple days and did next to nothing. What's your excuse?"

Instead of answering, the prisoner stretches out on the cot and sighs. "You don't need to be here, you know."

"Yeah." She gives up on her current piece and picks up a new one. "You've mentioned that. Multiple times."

"No, I mean you just admitted this is a waste of time. 's not like you have a lot of that left either. Why are you here?"

"Why are you?"

The prisoner snorts. "Not like I have much of a—"

"You weren't really trying to kill me." The princess forces herself to turn and face her. She was planning on having this conversation later, but the prisoner's right. She's running out of time. "If you were, your hands would be around my throat right now. What are you actually—"

The prisoner's hands are suddenly around her throat. She'd expected that, though. And she has plenty of practice not flinching at sudden contact. The last Princess of Rosenly throws out her left elbow to brace herself just as she's knocked onto her back and does her best to let her boredom shine through as she stares up at the panting form above her. Tangled, unwashed curls keep coming dangerously close to landing in her mouth, but the princess doesn't let herself turn away. Instead, she meets wide, dark eyes head-on. "Out of your system yet?" she asks.

The prisoner grits her teeth. Her grip tightens. "I could—"

"There's a knife in my right boot."

"I—what?"

"There's a knife in my right boot," the princess repeats. "I'm not an idiot. I don't lock myself in cells with people who've tried to kill me unarmed. It's right beside the buckle. If you want to get this over with, slitting my throat would probably be faster."

The prisoner stares at her. She breathes. Then, she sighs, lets go, and rolls over to stare at the ceiling. "You're insane," she whispers.

The princess remains on her back, eyes tracing cracks in the ceiling. If she tries, she can almost pretend they're just two people in a field, enjoying the sky. "I'm dying," she acknowledges. "Makes it kind of hard to worry about death threats. Especially when you know the person threatening you won't see them through."

The prisoner groans. "How'd you know?"

"Something about your eyes, I think. Or the way your hands shook."

(Or the way they hadn't when she'd healed her)

"Shit," the prisoner says. "Well... just because I'm not a killer doesn't mean I don't want you dead."

"Yeah, I've noticed." The princess tries to laugh but something catches in her chest as she does. "Do you think you could pretend you don't?" she whispers. "Just... not all the time, but maybe at least tonight? And tomorrow night? Or... at least sometimes?" It's been a week. She doesn't know why she'd thought a week would make this girl suddenly like her, but she truly had.

(Hope is a very hard thing to kill in a princess, after all)

"Thought you didn't want me to lie."

"I don't!" she corrects. "I just..." she sighs. "I had a really rough day, okay? That's why... I'm never going to be late again now that I know how serious that is, but that's why I was. And it would be really helpful to have someone to—"

The prisoner flies to her feet. "I spend all day in a fucking cage."

"I know that!" The princess rushes to get up. "I just—"

"I've spent a *week* sitting in a fucking cage with no one to talk to but the princess who ruined the world who's actively trying to manipulate me! You left me in the dark after

I *told you* what it'd do and you're expecting me to ask about whatever passes for a rough day for a fucking—"

"You tried to kill me!" The last princess of Rosenly doesn't know where the anger comes from, but all at once, she's yelling.

And all at once, the prisoner's silent.

"You tried to kill me!" she repeats. If she doesn't, she already knows she'll lose her momentum. It's nice to feel in control for once. "And maybe you weren't actually going to do it and maybe even if you were you would have done a terrible job, but you did. You can't—you're a prisoner for skies' sake! You're supposed to be rotting away! You don't get to be mad at me for expecting you to ask before I give you baked goods when you're a prisoner and you tried to kill me and I'm still here! Every single night! Sleeping on a fucking floor because—"

"I never asked you to be here," the prisoner mutters.

"Well maybe I should have made you!" she exclaims. "Maybe if I'd made you beg, you'd be desperate enough to act like a human being for more than a second at a time instead of being an entitled fucking bitch just because you know *I'm* not a shitty enough person to leave you alone!" Her fists shake against her sides. She might be imagining it, but she's fairly certain her starlight starts to spin faster. "I have to stand there and *smile*!" she says. "All day! While strangers stick their tongues down my throat and their hands around my waist, I have to smile and kiss them back and then I have to *thank them*! I was just born, Sylvie! That's it! That's the big, terrible thing I did. You tried to kill me and the worst I've made you do is say please once or twice! You at least get to show when you're upset, so yeah, I think I actually am allowed to—" Just as quickly, the anger leaves her.

(The princess can never hold on to any kind of power for too long)

She catches herself breathless, mortified, and midsentence. "Sorry," she moves to sit against the un-barred wall, letting her eyes fall shut and her head drop to her chest. "You were already freaking out, I didn't mean to… like I said. Rough day." She feels someone sit down beside her and does her best to not flinch when an arm brushes against hers.

"Tell me about whatever passes for a rough day for a fucking princess."

The last princess of Rosenly's eyes snap open. She instantly shakes her head. "I didn't mean to… you don't actually have to be nice to me. I didn't want to—that was the point, actually. That you don't have to. I didn't want to… I need you to have a choice."

The prisoner rolls her eyes. "I'm not being nice, I'm being nosy."

"But you said…"

She shrugs. "Changed my mind. It gets boring down here, okay? So just… tell me, then don't leave next time I'm being a dick."

"I don't need to let you insult me for decisions I didn't even get to make," she says. "That's—"

"I'll stick to the ones you did then, okay?" the prisoner says. "Is that… can that be enough?"

She doesn't want her to leave, the princess realizes. She'd already known she didn't want her to put out the light, of course, but now the prisoner doesn't want her specifically to leave. She bites her lip to keep from smiling but the prisoner misreads it.

"Look," she says. "You're right. I tried to kill you and you're being freakishly decent about it, so I shouldn't…" she sighs. "I'm an ass. I'm going to keep being an ass, but maybe it's not fair to be a dick about laws made when you were a kid. I can try to be a bit more decent about that specifically. Just…" She scratches at the back of her neck. "Stars, Princess, just hurry up and tell me about your day so we can stop talking about this, yeah?"

"It'd be more proper to call me Your Highness, actually. If you're trying to be decent. -er."

The prisoner snorts. "I might be able to acknowledge you're not the absolute worst, but I'm never gonna respect you enough to call you that. Give me a name and I'll actually use it, though. Probably."

She searches for one and comes up empty. Her original name was chosen to honour the stars, long before her parents realized how risky forcing wishes could truly be. She's fairly certain she's had no name at all since she was eight. That feels slightly too pathetic to admit though, so she goes for another uncomfortable truth instead. "They're widening the kissing line age range again," the princess whispers. "To fifty."

The prisoner waits a long beat before responding. "And you're… upset about that."

"I know I shouldn't be," she instantly corrects. "I get I should be thankful. And I am, obviously. So many people are willing to waste their entire day—sometimes multiple days—waiting in line just on the off chance they might be the one whose kiss would—"

"No, that makes sense," the prisoner rescues her.

She freezes. "It does?"

"Not like I'd want dozens of strangers shoving their tongues down my throat either."

"But—"

The prisoner leans towards her. Their shoulders almost touch. Almost, but not quite. "Don't worry. Shittalk as many of your people as you want. 'S not like there's anyone I can tell."

She shakes her head. "I *am* thankful though," she insists. "Usually. But the first few days after we increase the age limit are always... they're horrible." She hears her own voice waver and break and can do nothing to stop it.

(Princesses worthy of saving rarely get to stop anything at all)

"It's..." she hugs her knees tighter, threading her fingers together as if that will somehow trap her pulse. "I know most people are trying to help and it'd be terrible to accuse them of anything else, but the first few days after... there's a certain kind of person who rushes to be first in line every time we open it further." All at once, the last princess of Rosenly's voice becomes calm, even, and clear. Like any well-trained princess, there's a threshold to her discomfort. Once she passes it, it's second nature to block herself out. "They grab," she says. "They grab too much and they hold too tight and they take too long to let go and they... I don't like the grabbing. I really, really don't like the grabbing. And I know there's going to be more of it than usual these next few days and I can't... I really don't want to go out tomorrow. Which I know is terrible of me!" she quickly adds. "I get that, but—"

"That's shitty."

"I know!" she insists. "I'm sorry, I shouldn't have—"

"No, Princess," A palm presses against her knee. "That's really, really shitty, okay?"

She stares. "It is?"

"It is." The prisoner lets go. "You do know you're in charge of an entire kingdom though, right? Can't you just make a no touching rule? Or impose some kind of time limit?"

(Strangers don't save princesses who are picky)

"Strangers don't save princesses who are picky," she says.

"Yeah. And strangers who think telling them where and how they can touch you makes you 'picky' definitely aren't going to be able to save you anyway."

"Shut up!" she jolts. "They could be. There's still a chance—"

"Do you actually want them to be?"

She doesn't know how she's supposed to respond, so she doesn't. The prisoner's also silent. Then, she kicks herself to her feet and walks over to the puzzle. She returns with a piece stuck between her middle and index finger.

"Here," she says. "Border piece. It goes near the corner closest to the cot."

The princess frowns, confused. "It only took you a few seconds to figure that out?"

"Course not. If I was that good, It'd be done by now. I just…" She sighs, sitting back down. "It was already attached. I took it off. Seemed like you could use some kind of win."

She almost laughs. "I'm not so pathetic that—"

"Do you want the piece or not?"

She snatches it. "Obviously I want it." She marches over to the puzzle and quickly finds exactly where the prisoner removed it from. When she turns back around, the prisoner's staring at her uncomfortably.

"I umm… when I tried to kill you," the prisoner offers. "I grabbed you. A lot. I didn't mean to… I'm sorry. I didn't know."

The last princess of Rosenly squints. "That's… you're apologizing for that and not the attempted murder?"

She shrugs. "That was political. Wasn't about you. Probably could've done it with a bit less physical contact, though."

"And you're… also not apologizing for tackling me a bit ago? And trying to suffocate me?"

The prisoner rolls her eyes. "Stars, Princess. Learn how to accept an apology. Of course I'm not. You very clearly goaded me into that." But her eyes aren't on the princess's neck or even on the spot on her stomach that she forced against herself last week. They're on her left hand. The one she pulled against her face earlier that evening.

The princess swallows, mouth abruptly incredibly dry. "I forgive you, then," she says. "For that."

"Good. Then I forgive you for trying to weaponize pastries against me."

"That's not—"

The prisoner holds up a hand to silence her. "No time, Princess. We've got a puzzle to solve."

"We've…" she tries to quell it. "You mean together?"

(Hope is a very hard thing to kill in a princess, after all)

The prisoner shrugs. "You're in here, aren't you? Don't see why you would be if you weren't gonna help."

"And you're… okay with that?"

She rolls her eyes. "Just shut up and do the fucking puzzle."

The last princess of Rosenly knows it's supposed to offend her, but she feels the strange urge to thank her for that.

Sylvie

A dungeon is a difficult place to avoid impatience, but as she waits for the princess the next night, Sylvie finds it even more difficult than usual to sit still. Her every nerve desperately urges her towards movement; a survival instinct intent on keeping her from having too much time to think.

Last night was different. Instead of staring at her with a vague sense of mourning until one of them eventually managed to fall asleep, the princess stayed in her cell, trying and failing to finish the puzzle until she was physically too exhausted to keep her eyes open a moment longer. Sylvie hadn't known how to get her to stop.

(She'd been all too aware of how desperately a body attempts to distract itself from confronting horrible truths to dare try to)

They barely talked. When they did, it was mostly argumentative.

(She can never help herself)

But last night, the princess was there and real and solid and doing a terrible job preventing herself from crying.

Rosenly's princess's sadness is infamous. She's been a tragic, doomed little girl hurtling herself toward death for as long as Sylvie can remember. Her mere existence has spawned countless mournful poems and haunting ballads. But there's a difference between true sadness and tragedy.

Before, the princess had been an elusive symbol. A bedtime story. A blight.

Now, she is a girl with too-long arms and too sparse hair and haunting, forlorn eyes. Now, she is a person who's ridiculously inept at puzzles. She's the key to a salvation Sylvie's done nothing to earn, but one that she knows she's inevitably going to seize regardless.

71

(She can never help herself)

Now, she is the girl with too-long arms and too-sparse hair & an ineptitude at puzzles who Sylvie needs to trick into believing she might genuinely be able to save. Guilt claws at her, but it never catches. Or maybe it does. Maybe enough guilt's already torn her to shreds that fresh ones have nothing left to sink into.

The hidden door creaks open before the sun's even begun to recede. The night before the princess had been well rested and dreading something that hadn't even happened yet and she still managed to be late, but Sylvie didn't consider for a moment that she might be tonight. Not because they're anywhere close to friends or because she's tricked herself into believing that the princess cares about her specifically, but because every day she's forced to accept more and more that this girl is not her parents. She does not make promises to break them.

"I'm here!" the princess calls well before coming into view. It confirms what Sylvie's already guessed. There's no guard at the end of the tunnel. There wouldn't be any point to the secrecy if there was. If Sylvie manages to convince the princess to become careless enough, there'll be no one waiting to stop her escape.

She's allowed to want this. Her role was to get caught, not to remain prisoner. She might be of even more help if she escapes.

(And she's scared)

(And she's desperate)

"I'm here!" the princess repeats. "I'm not late."

Sylvie grimaces. Guilt reaches for her again. It finds nothing.

Sylvie Castell has always been selfish and right now, what she wants more than anything is to keep herself from ever being trapped in the dark again. Even if it means manipulating a princess just desperate enough for a chance at survival to make the mistake of believing that Sylvie might give her it.

The princess is in such a rush to get through the door that she practically trips over her skirts as she does, but once she's in the dungeon, she freezes, stares, then quickly turns and busies herself with the lamp. When she finally approaches the bars her eyes might be clear, but the bruises beneath them are visibly redder than usual. Sylvie's been rapidly learning that she has no idea how to act in the presence of a princess's tears.

"Hi," the princess eventually speaks. "How umm…"

"You gave me a shit puzzle."

"I'm—excuse me?"

"The puzzle," Sylvie sweeps an arm over it. It took her all day to complete it, but the princess doesn't need to know that. "I finished it. It's missing four pieces. That's what, another thinly veiled manipulation tactic? I'm supposed to beg you to hand them over?"

"No!" the princess exclaims. "I didn't…" she frowns. "You're in a cell. How did you manage to lose multiple pieces?"

"You clearly never gave them to me!"

The princess clicks her tongue and pulls out her ring of keys. Sylvie taps her nails against her side as realization sets in. If she was someone more strategic, there'd be some kind of plan involved here. She's lured the most protected person in the kingdom into her cell for the second time in two days, and this time, she's done it on purpose. And supposedly, she knows exactly where the princess keeps her weapon.

There might not be a guard at the top of the stairs, but there are some throughout the castle. If she's right, the tunnel must be connected to the outside world, but she's nowhere near desperate enough to risk trying to navigate that on her own yet. Sylvie hasn't tricked the princess into her cell as an act of self-preservation, she's done it because she's terrified she'll start crying again. Knowing that disgusts her.

(Or at least, it should)

The princess goes straight to her cot and kicks it over with the toe of her slipper. "Well, there's one," she narrates, bending down to collect it. She grabs the entire mattress as she stands back up, shaking it out to reveal two more pieces. She turns around to glare. "You had all day. Did you honestly not even bother—" She stops moving mid-sentence. Then, her shoulders fall. "Where's the fourth piece?" she mumbles.

"Well if I *knew*, I obviously would've—"

"I'm not an idiot!"

Sylvie freezes. She's never been particularly well-versed in anticipating the emotions of others, but genuine, explosive anger was not something she'd accounted for here. "I don't—"

"I'm not—I'm so sick and tired of everyone acting like I'm some kind of helpless child!"

"Wait, that's not—"

The princess's attention snaps to Sylvie. She thought she'd been yelling at her, but it seems almost as if she's only just remembered that Sylvie's even there. She flings the pieces in her fist to the floor and storms toward her.

Sylvie's not good at standing her ground so much as she's typically terrible at knowing when she shouldn't, but she's still so thrown by the tonal shift that as the princess corners her against the wall, she allows herself to back into it. The princess plants a palm on either side of her shoulders, trapping her in place.

"I let strangers do whatever they want to my body every single day," she hisses. "I've spent years letting them. And I say exactly what they want me to and react exactly how they want me to and I don't complain or flinch or—I might not be the most informed person in the entire kingdom, but I haven't been a child for years now." The princess stares directly at her. Even if her irises weren't ringed in light, Sylvie has a feeling she wouldn't be able to look away. "I'm smarter and tougher and *far* more mature than anyone ever gives me credit for, and I don't need a failed assassin, of all people, acting like I'm so *stupid* that I wouldn't realize—"

"You're not," Sylvie manages to blink just long enough to remember how to speak.

"—that you *clearly* hid things intentionally just to give yourself an excuse to—"

"I was trying to be nice!" she finally remembers to explain.

"—act like—what?" the princess freezes.

Sylvie sucks on her cheek. She looks away. "I umm…" she mumbles. "I was trying to be nice. I guess."

"By yelling at me? And accusing me of trying to manipulate you?"

"Well, I never said I was good at it," she mutters. "You did, actually. That first night. Bet you feel pretty ridiculous now, huh?"

The princess just blinks. "In what world was that—"

"You were having a shit day," Sylvie says. "I knew that. And I also knew I'd probably be awful company afterward but that you'd force yourself to stay anyway because that's how you work so I…" she sighs. "I'm stuck in a cell, Princess. I couldn't fix your shit day and stars know it'll take a lot longer than a single day to fix me, but I could hide enough pieces to maybe let you feel like you were accomplishing something after you found them, okay? Which was clearly stupid, so…"

"You were trying to be… nice?"

"Yeah."

"To… me?"

"Evidently."

The princess starts to smile. "That's progress, right? That feels like progress. Oh," her eyes widen. "Did I just ruin it? By yelling at you?"

Sylvie rolls her eyes. "I don't think so, believe it or not."

"Okay," she nods. "Good. That's good."

She doesn't move.

Neither does Sylvie. "Umm, Princess?"

"Mmhmm?"

"Still kinda trapped here."

"Oh!" She jumps away instantly. "Sorry, I didn't mean to… I wasn't trying to scare you. I wanted to make you listen, but I shouldn't have—"

"I tried to kill you," Sylvie reminds her. "You're allowed to occasionally be a little unhinged back." She tries to cross back to her cot, but the princess keeps talking.

"Still, I shouldn't have… I'm sorry. Stars, you were trying to be nice and I—"

"How'd today go?" Sylvie doesn't mean to be cruel, she just wants to get her to stop apologizing. It's just the question at the front of her mind.

But it is. *She* is. Because the princess looks right at her, opens her mouth to respond, then abruptly begins to sob.

"Shit," Sylvie stumbles back into the wall as the princess falls to her knees. She's never been good with tears. They've always made her reckless, and this girl's more than most. "Shit, I umm…" she slowly walks around her before

awkwardly kneeling to join her on the floor. "Did you umm…
am I supposed to hug you or something?" She regrets the
offer as soon as she makes it. Hugs are awkward and
unknowable and far too intimate for Sylvie's liking. She's
given very few, but she's still certain she's somehow uniquely
terrible at them.

Luckily, the princess instantly says, "No!"

But Sylvie's relief is short-lived, because after a
moment she adds, "I think I might… could I hug you,
though?"

Sylvie frowns. "I thought you said—"

"Don't do it back," the princess sniffles. "Don't try to
comfort me or touch me or… or move too much or…"

"Okay." Sylvie awkwardly shuffles forward. "Okay."
The princess wraps her arms around her back and Sylvie goes
stiff as a board—she's as terrible a hug receiver as she is a
hug giver—but the princess is either too distraught or too
desperate to notice, because she doesn't let go. Instead, she
melts into Sylvie's shoulder blade, smearing tears and snot
against the dirt-and-blood-stained blouse Sylvie's already
been wearing for over a week. Instead, she latches her fingers
around her own wrists and squeezes so tightly that Sylvie's
certain she must be able to feel every single one of her
heartbeats, so she tries to focus on slowing them down.
Instead, she pours all her grief and anguish over Sylvie and
refuses to let go until she's run out of energy for sobs and
resorted instead to a gentle shaking.

And Sylvie welcomes it. Sylvie hasn't gotten the
opportunity to feel useful for a very, very long time. Staying
still seems such a simple thing that even she won't be able to
mess it up, so of course she welcomes it.

By the time the princess's grip goes slack, Sylvie
can't tell if she's even still awake. Slowly, she squirms her

way out of the embrace and turns just in time to brace the princess's fall when her absence causes her to topple. She helps her lower herself to the ground, then flops onto her own back to stare at the ceiling.

(If she squints enough, she can almost pretend the shadows flickering against it are starlight)

"I shouldn't have done that," the princess eventually whispers.

"No." Sylvie shakes her head, though she knows the princess isn't looking anywhere near her. "Don't do that. You're fine."

"I'll bring you a new shirt tomorrow."

She snorts at the practicality of it. "Good. Honestly, Princess! You've got a whole castle at your disposal! Kind of offended you didn't offer earlier."

"I would've, if you'd asked for the pie."

Sylvie bites her lip to smother a laugh. "Of course you would've. Maybe I'll actually have to next time, then." She considers. "I umm… I don't think I'd be able to, actually," she forces herself to admit. Even that scrapes its way up her throat, leaving a slight sting against her vocal cords. "Not because you're a princess or because I'm in denial about relying on you for things because trust me, I'm far too aware of that part, I've just never been good at it. Asking for things. From anyone. Even doing this much is… a lot."

"I'll bring pie," the princess nods. "Tomorrow."

Sylvie smiles. "I prefer tarts, actually."

"Then I'll bring tarts." She hears her draw a long breath followed by an even longer sigh. "Today was bad," the princess whispers. "Today was really, really bad."

"I know," Sylvie says. "I'm sorry."

She rolls over to face her. "Are you?"

"Of course. Thought we agreed I wouldn't lie to make you feel better."

The princess doesn't respond.

Sylvie sighs. "What should I do? If I wanted to actually do something to make it less shitty?"

"Distract me?"

She smiles ruefully. "Yeah, that didn't really go the best last time I tried."

The princess is quiet for another moment, then, she shifts slightly closer. "I'm not a weaver, am I? You acted like... but I'm not just human either. Do you know what..."

Sylvie frowns as she trails off. "You really don't know?"

"A lot of people spend a lot of time protecting me from difficult or dangerous things," she whispers.

"Yet they leave you alone in cells with people who've tried to kill you?"

The princess smiles. "Already told you. You did a terrible job. Clearly you're no threat."

"Maybe I'm trying to lull you into a false sense of security."

The princess rolls her eyes. Sylvie doesn't think she's ever seen a princess do that before.

And so, she says, "you're a wish. Obviously."

She waits for understanding to dawn, but it doesn't.

"Like from the stories?" she prompts. "A child born from the stars? That's kind of the whole—"

"There are no stories," the princess interrupts. "I've read them all. There aren't any about people like me."

Sylvie squints at her. "You think you've read *every* story?"

The princess blushes and looks away. "I'm a princess," she mutters. "I'm supposed to be spoiled. I could've—"

"There are *hundreds* of stories about the stars, Princess. Banning them doesn't stop them from existing."

"Oh." The princess just watches her.

Sylvie groans. "I'm supposed to tell you one now, aren't I? If I'm trying to be… civil?"

"You don't have to," the princess says instantly. "But…"

"But?"

"You asked how to distract me, didn't you?"

She sighs, shifting against the floor to get more comfortable. "Once upon a time…"

The Last Princess of Rosenly

"Once upon a time, there lived a farmer and his wife," the prisoner begins to recite.

The last princess of Rosenly squeezes her eyes shut. She focuses on steadying her breathing. If she tries desperately enough, she can almost stop herself from rubbing her tongue against her molars where the ghosts of a thousand other tongues still sit despite her useless attempts to scrub them away. She might be alone in a cell with a near stranger who's already tried to kill her, but at least this stranger doesn't seem to want to kiss her at all, despite the ample opportunity she's had to. Despite the fact that the princess is supposed to want her to.

She's safe.

"This was long ago, of course. When wishes were accidents and skies were dark and endless."

The prisoner's voice is gruffer than the princess is used to. Perhaps that's come from the dungeon, but she suspects it was the distance that's done it. The air in the castle sometimes feels too light to breathe. Maybe it gets thicker, the further away you grow up. Maybe the prisoner's vocal cords had the opportunity to grow stronger.

"But once upon a time, there lived a farmer and his wife, and once upon a time, they craved not a bountiful harvest nor riches nor gold, but a child to call their own."

The princess's breath catches. She's been brought up on fairy tales

(they're her birthright)

but never this one. The princesses of her childhood grew up just as doomed and tragic as she had, but never in the exact same way. She knew others had, of course, but tragic mistakes cease to be tragic mistakes once they're repeated, so all tales of other children born of the stars left Rosenly the moment she arrived.

Yet the prisoner recites it as casually as a greeting.

"I can stop."

She opens her eyes when the prisoner's tone abruptly changes, the hitch in her breath having apparently been audible enough to interrupt her.

The last princess of Rosenly shakes her head.

"I didn't mean to… tell me if you need me to stop, okay? I know other stories."

This time, she fights to keep her breathing even. It's barely an offer at all, but to the last princess of Rosenly, it's everything.

(Princesses worthy of saving rarely get to stop anything at all)

"Okay," she whispers through shaking lips. It's the best she can manage. She lets her eyes fall shut again and eventually, the story continues.

"Though modest in wealth and land," the prisoner says, "the farmer and his wife were rich in love. The farmer would go door to door in town, distributing his crops to those who needed more 'til there was scarcely enough left for himself. The wife would open her hearth and heart to any poor soul who needed a dry place to rest their head. All who met the couple knew they'd been created to nurture, yet no child ever came." The prisoner pauses.

If it's to look at her, at least the princess doesn't have to witness it.

"And so," she starts back up. "they began to wish. Little was known of wishing back then. Occasionally, a desperate soul would want something desperately enough at the exact right moment to tether a star in the skies, but human eye could not yet see the threads of starlight, so wishing was rarely intentional. Weavers didn't exist yet, so there was no one to ensure their hopes and dreams would be heard.

"The farmer and his wife possessed no child, but they had an entire town mourning for them. And so, one night, when enough wishes lined up at the exact right moment, a single star decided to take pity on them. Creating life from nothing requires a greater miracle than even the stars could summon on their own, so that star decided to become the life herself. Detaching herself from the sky, she descended to the earth and nestled herself safely in the woman's womb.

"When the first wish was born, no one knew she was a wish at all. She was a child with hair and eyes of gold and skin that shone through even the darkest of nights. Were she born to any other parents she might have grown up spoiled and vain…"

The prisoner pauses again and this time, the princess is certain it's to look at her. So, the last princess of Rosenly blindly juts out her foot, smiling to herself when she feels it connect with leg.

The prisoner cackles. Then, she continues. "But the farmer and his wife were good, modest people, so she grew to be every bit as humble and lovely as them. When she was twelve, however, the girl began to wilt."

The last princess of Rosenly flinches. She hears the prisoner move.

"Still okay?" she checks.

The princess nods.

"The girl began to wilt," she reorients herself in the story. "Stars weren't meant to be confined to the earth, you see. Hers began to grow restless. Physicians from across the land came to tend to her, but none could determine what had caused her sudden decline.

"and so, the people turned to wishing again, despite not knowing how much power that truly held. No one knows if it was another wish catching or perhaps the girl's own star taking pity on her, but one morning when her parents went to check on her, they found the girl full of the unbounded joy they'd worried they'd lost forever. While she slept, her starlight had whispered the truth to her. She was a wish. The very first one. A child not meant to exist. It was nearing time for her to go home.

"Were she born to any other parents, the wish might have embraced the chance to return to the skies forevermore, but the farmer and his wife were good, modest people, and she knew her departure would break their hearts.

"And so, the girl bargained. She told her starlight of the wonders of humanity and the star agreed that if she could share humanity's prized possession with her—a kiss of true, pure, unending love—then she might be persuaded to stay. Starlight requires tethering, after all. And what better thing to tether it than true love?

"It took less than a month, of course. The First Wish was every bit as humble and lovely as her parents, so suitors came from all across the land to try their chance at kissing her. She married an equally lovely farmhand from an equally lovely family and the two lived in happiness and bliss for the rest of her earthly days. The end."

The princess's eyes fly open. "That's it?"

"That's it."

"Is that the truth or a fairytale?"

"I'm not sure people knew the difference, back then."

She sits up, hugging her knees to her chest. "I don't think fairytales should end with twelve-year-olds getting married," she whispers.

"That's…" the prisoner slowly rises to match her. "A good point, actually. That's probably not the actual end anyway since weavers still exist, right? We're descendants of wishes. It's why we can spin starlight."

"What does it look like?"

"String, mostly. But more… thicker and thinner at the same time."

She smiles slightly. "That doesn't make any sense."

"No," the prisoner agrees. "I think the stars love things that don't."

The last princess of Rosenly runs her tongue along her teeth. She tastes her gums. "Why do you hate me so much, then?"

The prisoner looks away. "I umm… I don't…"

"Not me specifically," she clarifies. She's too scared to let her finish the sentence. "Or you specifically, really. If wishes are the reason weavers even exist, why do you… you called me an abomination."

The prisoner sighs. "I shouldn't have," she says. "You were right. You didn't ask to be born, that's not…" She traces circles into the dirt with her thumb. "We vowed to never help anyone wish for life," she explains. "Decades ago. If it somehow happens on its own that's one thing, but the stars don't… they never want it. It's always forced. It's less weaving, more tangling and even then, you need to amass a small army of wishers and weavers to make it work. Stars don't want to be trapped on the ground, Princess. It's cruel. That's not… that's a good thing though, okay?" she says. "It means somewhere deep down, you want to go back to the sky. If you have to in a few weeks, maybe the earth just wasn't good enough for you. Maybe for some wishes, there's just nothing down here that can compete with being pure starlight."

The princess sucks on her lip, considering. "Do you think I'll still exist?" she risks asking. "Once I go back to the stars? I'm—I don't remember anything from before. What if the only parts of me that feel like me are the human parts? Do you know if... what happens to me?"

"I don't know," the prisoner admits.

The princess knew the disappointment was coming, but when it slams against her chest, she's still not prepared for it.

"But," the prisoner offers. "I do know the stars like people. They're fascinated by us. And you used to be one of them, right? So if anything, they're probably even more invested in you. I don't think... I don't think they'd want you to just stop being."

"I talked to them once." It's meant to be a thought, but the last princess of Rosenly is too exhausted to contain it to her brain. Even after hearing her own voice, though, she's still half convinced she hasn't spoken at all. The prisoner isn't reacting nearly as much as she should be to that.

"Oh," she says.

"You don't believe me. In your story, wishes are able to—"

"Sometimes wishes happen on their own. Maybe you just got lucky."

"I *didn't*," she insists. "I was..." she scrunches up her nose as she attempts to surface the long-suppressed memory. "Eight, I think. I must've been. It would've been right after my parents got frustrated enough that I hadn't found my true love yet to do something about it. Weaving had only been illegal for a few weeks, but weavers were already furious. A group of them kidnapped me, did you know that?" She watches the prisoner as attentively as she can, but she just rolls her eyes.

"Yes, princess. A kidnapped royal isn't the kind of thing you can avoid hearing about, even when you're also just a kid."

"Oh," she says.

"That must've been—sorry. I didn't mean to… that must've been scary. Was the constellation that took you—"
"I don't remember anything about them." She's been through this line of questioning too many times to count. "They were fine, I think. Just kept me in a room the whole time. I don't think I was processing much of it, I umm… I think I just spent most of it sobbing."

The prisoner smiles slightly. "Sounds like you."

"You're supposed to be playing nice!"

"This is me doing that!"

Strangely, the princess finds herself resisting the urge to grin back at that. "I could see them, though," she continues explaining. "The stars. Their roofs are all glass, you know. They—"

"Princess," she interrupts. "Weaver, remember? I know."

The last princess of Rosenly feels herself blush. "Right. Right, well I could see the stars? And I didn't know enough about wishes yet to know I wasn't supposed to talk to them—I knew pretty much nothing about wishes at all, actually—and I was scared and confused and just wanted to go back home, so I asked them to send me there. Out loud. And they *moved*, Sylvie. Right away. That's how they found me. I asked them to, then the stars started to *move*." She chews on her lip. "It wasn't chance. It wasn't a coincidence. I swear for half a moment I could even see the thread. Do you think… my parents hate the stars. I'm supposed to too, I think. They think they only gave me to them to hurt them. They think now that they're all gone, they might forget to take me back. But do you think… they like me, I think. They helped me. It's supposed to be nearly impossible for a wish to connect without a weaver, right? So they must have. If… if we still had some here. If I told them I wanted to stay. Then do you think… would they let me?"

"Run away with me," the prisoner immediately suggests. "They probably won't listen to you on your own, they might not listen to me either, but at least they'd hear me. We can go somewhere full of stars and talk to them together."

The princess suppresses a sigh. She should have seen this coming. This girl is not her friend, she's her captive.

She's apparently incapable of suppressing anything at all around the prisoner, though, because she notices.

"Hey," the prisoner says softly. Or as close to softly as she seems capable of. "You can't get pissed at me for trying, Princess. I'm probably never going to stop."

"I know," she acknowledges.

"Doesn't mean I think you're terrible company or anything. I even offered to let you tag along."

"Because you'd need me to let you out!"

"Still offered," the prisoner shrugs.

She rolls her eyes. "Why didn't you leave already?" she realizes. "When the stars started to disappear, if it's truly so terrible being without them, you could've—"

The prisoner's eyes narrow. She's asked the wrong thing. "Rosenly's stars are mine," she spits. "They're the ones I was born under. I won't abandon them just because some royal assholes decided they're not."

The princess flinches.

"You're not the assholes," she corrects. "In this specific instance."

"No, I'm just the assholes' child."

"Yes," the prisoner nods. "Exactly." Her expression softens. "Seriously, though. I'd rather some inferior stars than a dungeon and you clearly don't like being here either. If we left—"

"If we left my parents would lose their minds," she stops her.

The last princess of Rosenly's considered it before, of course. It would've been impossible not to. She's running out of life, yet she's lived absolutely none of it.

"I'm a princess," she reminds them both. "The only one. If you think they're too quick to persecute now, what do you think would happen if I just disappeared?"

The prisoner studies her knuckles. "You've been thinking about it, then."

"Of course I have." She always is. She's never not. "Rosenly's my kingdom, though. Whether or not I ever actually inherit it. My existence has already wreaked more than enough havoc. I can't cause anymore."

She's expecting the prisoner to continue to push, but she just nods.

"Where's the fourth piece?" the princess remembers.

"Under the dinner tray. Not many hiding spots in here."

In silence, the last princess of Rosenly finishes the puzzle. She doesn't feel triumphant or successful once it's been completed, she feels nothing at all. "I could go get something else," she offers. "If you're bored. Or need anything. Not too much—I've officially never been down here so anything I leave needs to be believably part of some kind of deal, but I could."

The prisoner glares. "Thought we said you weren't gonna keep making me ask for things."

"I'm not trying to," the princess chews at her lip. "I'm just... I don't get a lot of spare time. I don't know what people usually fill it with. It'd be helping me more than helping you, actually. If you came up with something."

She watches the prisoner consider, breath lodged halfway up her throat. The last princess of Rosenly needs something to do. She's spent far too much of her life not doing.

"Know any games?" the prisoner's eyes flick up to hers.

"Yes!" Relief carries her to her toes. "We used to play checkers when I was younger. When we were still taking our time with suitors. I probably have a board in a closet somewhere."

Technically, the princess was taught how to lose checkers, not how to play it, but she figures winning will be even easier to master.

The prisoner nods. "Go grab it, then. Bring something you're worse at tomorrow, though. If... distractions might be helpful, I think."

"Distractions might be helpful," she exhales.

The princess exits and relocks the cell. Before pulling open the door to the tunnel, however, she hesitates.

"Will it be terrible, Sylvie?" she asks. The words require so much courage that she has none left to turn and face her. "Whatever you're actually here for? Whatever they're planning?"

"I have no idea what—"

"Just—please. Will it be terrible?"

The prisoner's silent for so long that the last princess of Rosenly almost manages to turn. And then,

"No, Princess. If it would be, I wouldn't... no."

Her chest caves as she exhales. Her shoulders shrink.

She goes to find a game.

Sylvie

There are few things more certain to end in disaster than befriending a princess.

Sylvie's supposed to hate her. Partially because her mere existence is the product of bribery, coercion, and broken oaths, partially because that existence has already ruined her life in every conceivable way, but mostly because if she can't hate the princess, the only one left to hate is herself.

Sylvie already hates herself, of course.

(She can never help herself)

It was one of the first things she learned how to do. But it'd been easier, somehow, when she'd had someone else to hold responsible.

She's only here to weaken the castle's defenses. In a couple of weeks, the rest of her constellation will come.

(If they're actually coming)

In a couple of weeks, the princess will realize exactly why Sylvie agreed to get herself thrown in the dungeon in the first place, so in a couple of weeks, the princess is going to hate her. She might have been able to look past attempted murder, but she'll never forgive this. Sylvie knows it in the way her shoulders shake anytime either of them falls silent for too long. She sees it in the red, splotchy patches around her eyes that spread with every passing day and her ever-bleeding lips.

Sylvie hadn't meant to lie. She never would have willingly signed on to a plan she truly thought was cruel. But the more time she spends around the princess, the more certain she becomes that their definitions of cruelty vastly differ.

The princess is going to hate her, and knowing that's already making her far more uncomfortable than it should.

But above all else, Sylvie knows this is certain to end in disaster because the princess is dying. Sylvie might be too if her constellation doesn't come for her, but she hasn't had time to worry about that yet.

(She does constantly)

Her death is only a possibility. The princess's is inevitable. And Sylvie's too much of a coward to destroy the illusion that it might not be.

Luckily, Sylvie isn't befriending a princess. She spends every night that next week listening to her talk or cry or pretend she wants to do neither. She spends every day worrying herself sick and trying to anticipate all the ways she might be able to heal the wounds the princess will inevitably return to her with. But she's not befriending a princess. She's been careful to avoid any mentions of friendship, and until either of them do, she can at least rest in the safety of telling herself that's not what they're building together night after night. Sylvie intends to keep living in blissful denial for as long as she can.

Then, the princess wins a round of cards and doesn't say a word.

Sylvie frowns. The princess has gotten great at gloating over the course of their time together. Sylvie's trained her in it. She hadn't seemed any more distressed than usual when she'd entered the dungeon, but now, she's abruptly quiet.

She redeals. They begin again. Sylvie wins.

Sylvie never wins.

If she was truly doomed—if they really were friends after all—Sylvie would call her out on that and demand to know what's bothering her, but she isn't and they can't be, so she doesn't.

The princess redeals the cards. Her hands physically tremble as she does, but Sylvie will not destroy herself by asking why. She has always been selfish. It should be easy to keep being that here.

She loses again and when Sylvie looks up the princess refuses to meet her eye, but she just bites her tongue. If the princess wants to talk, she will. She's under no obligation to ask. The more she learns about the princess the messier things become, so she'll simply say nothing at all for the rest of the night and remain unscathed.

When the princess wordlessly picks up the cards to reshuffle, she squeezes too tightly and sends them shooting out around the cell.

"Sorry," she flies to her feet to collect them, brushing hair away from her face. "Sorry, I didn't mean to—"

Sylvie follows her. She's gotten too good at following her.

(She can never help herself)

She begins to reach for her arm then thinks better of it and stuffs her fist into her pocket. "Something's wrong with you," she declares.

She promised herself she wouldn't ask, after all.

The princess forces a laugh. "Well, I'm kind of dying, so—"

"Princess. What's wrong?"

(She promised herself she wouldn't ask)

"It's nothing," the princess says.

"It's very clearly not. And I'm kind of depending on you for like... basically everything right now, so if something's going to jeopardize that, you should—"

"It won't."

"Oh," Sylvie says.

(She promised herself she wouldn't ask)

"Tell me anyway?" she says. "If you want?"

The princess stares at her for a long moment before moving to sit on the cot. Sylvie takes it as her cue to follow.

(She's gotten too good at following her)

The princess picks at her nails. "I talked to my parents about you," she whispers. "Days ago. I wasn't supposed to tell you."

"Oh." Sylvie tries not to let her anxiety show visibly, but it doesn't work. Her heel pounds against the floor. "If it's… even if it's bad, I'd want you to tell me if—"

"You're going to be fine, Sylvie," the princess turns to face her. "No matter how this ends, you'll be fine, okay? Either I live and let you go as a show of good faith, or they do. I wasn't supposed to tell you. They're worried it'll disincentivize you from kissing me."

She shakes her head. "Your parents don't just let weavers go. They'll put out the light long enough to destroy me, then—"

"My parents need to mend their relationship with weavers after I'm gone," she interrupts. "What better way to do that than show that while their love for me led them to irrationality, they'd never let that push them far enough to hurt another child. It's a good story. And you're the only weaver younger than me they've ever imprisoned, so—"

"I'm actually a few—"

"Don't make me lie more than I have to for you."

Sylvie nods. Nothing about this makes sense, but she still nods. "Okay. Thank… how did you make them do that?"

She shrugs. "I'm dying. It's hard to refuse your child's only dying wish."

"You're wasting that on me?"

The princess smiles sadly. "I don't have anyone else to waste it on, Sylvie." She scoots closer. "I just… I need you to know you're safe no matter what, okay? Even if I'm not. Because I don't know why you're actually here and I know you're probably never going to tell me, but I do know that no matter what it is, I don't think you deserve to suffer."

"Okay," her throat goes dry. "I... thank you. Seriously."

The princess won't look at her. Her hands are still trembling.

(She promised herself she wouldn't ask)

"Are you going to tell me why you're actually—"

"Why do I?" the princess interrupts.

"What?"

She stares at her through tear-logged eyes. Sylvie swallows.

"Why do I deserve to suffer? I didn't *do* anything, Sylvie," she whispers. "I was just born. Why do you still think I... I wouldn't abandon you, you know. If you kissed me and it didn't work I wouldn't... I'd still be here, every single night. I'd still make sure nothing happens to you. If I did something to make you feel like I'd get mad if it didn't work—"

"You didn't," Sylvie stops her. No matter how desperately she wants to, she knows she can't keep forcing the princess to carry all her guilt. "I already knew that."

"Then why haven't you asked yet!" she exclaims. The princess closes her eyes. She takes a deep breath. She tears at her lip. "I knew you probably weren't going to fall in love with me," she says. "It's only been a couple of weeks. I'm not actually as naive as I'm supposed to be. But I thought you'd at least... I *worry* about you," she says. "I let myself start to *care* about you. Not just because you're probably the only person my age I haven't kissed yet, not just because you're the only one I get to even kind of pretend I'm actually responsible for, I let myself care about *you*. And you can't even... what could I have possibly done to make you hate me this much?"

It's supposed to be angry. From Sylvie, it would have come out angry.

(She can never help herself)

But from the princess, it's quiet, desperate, and vulnerable. As she stares at her and waits for a response, Sylvie realizes with a sickening horror that she's genuinely trying to ask a question.

"I don't—" her mouth is dry. Her lips are numb. She looks away. It's easier to face her, somehow, when she's not. Sylvie tangles her fingers together and studies those instead. "You don't deserve it, Princess. But sometimes the world isn't fair. It's..."

"I wasn't asking about the world, I was asking about you."

Sylvie swallows. "You know I don't hate you," she whispers.

(It's easier to speak in negatives)

"I'm..." she searches for some way to explain. "We're... I like it," Sylvie lands on. "When you're here. More than I do when you're not."

"Because you're bored," the princess says. "And you need me to be. Not—"

"I like it when *you're* here," she repeats. She risks glancing at her. "That's not... that's the best I can do for now, I think," she realizes. "Not because... I'm not as brave as you, okay? So that's all I can say. But I don't hate you," she reiterates. "I know you don't deserve to suffer."

"Then *why haven't you kissed me*?"

Sylvie freezes. She should have known. She never should have let herself ask. "You don't even like kissing," she tries to excuse it. "Why would I—"

"Because you know that," the princess's hands are suddenly wrapped around hers. It feels like a trap. Further confinement.

She desperately needs to pull away.

(She doesn't)

"Because you *know* it's destroying me." It's clearly an accusation, but the princess's voice doesn't raise, it shakes. "I come here every night broken and terrified and you still haven't… if you know how much I hate it, why haven't you tried to rescue me yet!"

It's too much. All at once, it's so much that she can no longer trust even her own spine to hold her.

Sylvie falls apart, the princess falls silent, and neither falls in love.

Sylvie

She already knew the princess thought they might be
soulmates. She's been encouraging it. Counting on it. At first
it had felt like the easiest way of protecting herself, then once
she'd learned that the princess wasn't the kind of person she
needed protecting from, she'd never bothered correcting her.

Because Sylvie's selfish. Because she's a coward.
Because she didn't want to have to know what would happen
to soft, kind eyes when you told them you'd never be able to
save them.

(She can never help herself)

But she'd never consider that the princess might
actually begin to like *her*. It had felt impossible. It should *be*
impossible. Girls reliant on falling in love shouldn't be able to
fall for girls incapable of ever doing the same.

She should have known better. People fall in love with
the wrong people all the time. She should have realized that
and told her before it was too late.

The princess likes her. The princess genuinely thinks
they might fall in love.

And Sylvie will *never love her back*.

She's hated almost every part of herself at one point
or another, but never this one. She took pride in it, once. It
made her less vulnerable. It meant there was one fewer way
she could be hurt. But not being able to fall in love has never
saved her from caring about people.

(She can never help herself)

And now, the first person who's been genuinely,
enthusiastically kind to her in years is going to die because of
feelings she'll never be able to reciprocate.

It seems the world's intent on picking out each and every part of Sylvie one by one just to hold them up to her face and show her how wrong they all are.

Sylvie doesn't cry when she's upset. That's always drawn too much attention. Her shoulders collapse and shake and her voice hitches, but she produces no tears.

But the princess notices the change, because of course she does. And so—because the princess is too benevolent for existence—soft warm hands find Sylvie's shoulders and gently push her back up.

"Hey," the princess is kneeling right in front of her now, worry clouding each and every one of her features. "It's okay, alright?" she says. "I'm sorry, I shouldn't have... there are plenty of reasons to not kiss a person, Sylvie. I know that. I didn't mean to yell at you."

"You didn't yell," she whispers. She's breathing too desperately for anything else. She loathes the smallness of it. It's always more difficult to pretend she's years away from childhood when she feels like crying. "At all, actually."

"Oh. Well then, I didn't mean to consider raising my voice at you."

Sylvie tries to laugh, but it's too difficult. Instead, she chokes.

The princess tries to smile. "You don't have to kiss me, okay?" she says. Because she'd offer up her own damnation on a silver platter if it'd make someone else more comfortable. And Sylvie is *killing her*. "Ever. I wouldn't make you."

"You need me to," she reminds them both.

"I don't," the princess shakes her head. "If it is you, I wouldn't want to force you into anything anyway, alright? I'd be... this is enough," she decides. "You've already saved me, okay? Because this last week's been... I've never gotten to beat someone at checkers."

It surprises Sylvie enough to allow her to actually snort this time.

The princess laughs lightly too. "This is enough." She repeats. She moves a hand around Sylvie's back to try and rub soft circles into it, but her fingers are tense and rigid.

Sylvie arches away. "Don't."

"What—"

"Don't touch me when you don't want to." She's spent two weeks with the princess as her sole companion. She knows how to recognize when she's uncomfortable.

The princess smiles again. That too is forced. "I upset you, Sylvie," she says. "I should—"

"Don't."

The princess's lips part slightly. She nods once. Then, she moves her hand to hover just beyond her jaw. "May I?"

Sylvie bows her head in assent.

The princess's fingers are fluid this time as she cups her cheek. Sylvie knows there are no tears beneath her eyes, but the princess brushes a finger over her skin regardless. "I'm glad you tried to kill me," she says.

Sylvie laughs.

"I am, though. It's... I don't get to know people who stay around, very often. I'm glad you did. Even if you didn't have a choice, I'm glad I got to..." she takes a deep breath. "That's more than enough for me. I promise."

It's tender and sweet and makes her every bone ache and Sylvie can offer none of that in return, so she responds with, "I'm not your true love, Princess."

The princess stiffens, but doesn't pull away. "And that's okay."

(It's not)

"If I thought I was," Sylvie attempts to explain. "Even if I didn't, actually. If I thought there was even a chance, I would've... I didn't avoid the line because I didn't want it to be me. It would've made things easier for everyone if it was. I never went because it would've been a waste of time. I don't like people. Like that."

"Oh," the princess's eyes widen slightly. Then, she laughs. "Stars, Sylvie! You could've just said that. I wouldn't have—"

"I know," Sylvie interrupts. "I should've told you the moment I realized you'd never be mad at me for that, but then I didn't and then you started to fall in love with me and—"

All at once the princess's hands are no longer on her skin. Not because she's scared her away, but because the princess is too busy falling backwards in a laughing heap.

Sylvie frowns. "What—" she blinks. "Are you, umm..."

It's some kind of mental break again, then. Like in the market. She moves off the cot to kneel over her.

"I'm sorry, Princess," she manages. "I never meant to—"

"You thought I was falling in *love* with you!" the princess gasps.

"But you said—"

"Stars, Sylvie!" She pushes herself back up against her palms. "I wanted you to want to kiss me because I wanted you to care enough to want me to survive, not—" She pauses to suck in more air. "You thought I was in love with you!"

"You were devastated I hadn't asked to kiss you!" Sylvie jumps to her own defense. "Obviously I..." she glares when the princess just keeps laughing. "You could be nicer about it, you know," she grumbles. "I was actually extremely emotionally distressed a few seconds ago, so—"

All at once, the princess freezes. She cocks her head to the side. "That's why I thought I was supposed to be making fun of you," she says. "You get uncomfortable when I try being nice. Which I fully intend to keep doing regardless of what you think, but I figured since you already seemed uncomfortable I should... was that wrong?"

Sylvie has never wanted to fall in love. Never even once. But for this girl, she wishes she could. She's known her for all of two weeks, and she already wishes she could.

"Sylvie?" the princess prompts. "You're umm... you're staring. Should I have not—"

"No," She shakes herself off. "No, no that was... I think I could actually hug you right now. If I didn't know you'd hate that."

"Oh!" The princess's eyes widen. "Yes, well... I helped, then?"

She smiles. "You helped, Princess."

(She always does)

The princess squeezes her hands. "It's a relief, in a way," she says. "That you just like men. I don't... I know I need a true love, but I think I might want a friend more. Not that—"

"We are." If she can let herself be known enough to comfort, surely she can let herself admit to friendship.

The princess grins. "Good. Well then, I'm glad. I'm sorry you let yourself feel guilty about that, Sylvie. Plenty of people only like men. I know you can't change that. It's fine."

"I don't like men."

"But you said—"

"I also don't like women," Sylvie explains. "I'm just not attracted to anyone."

"That doesn't make sense."

Sylvie doesn't know why—they *just* got back to feeling light and okay around each other again—but the princess physically flinches away from her.

"It's…" the princess scratches at her arm. "Maybe it really is you, then. Maybe you're confused. Everyone—"

"No," Sylvie says. "I'm pretty sure. Kinda spent my whole life living in this body, so—"

"That's not how it works!" the princess shouts. "It's…" she catches herself, slouching slightly and dropping her voice back down. She dons a plastered smile. "Everyone likes at least someone, Sylvie. Maybe you just haven't—"

Sylvie frowns. She's already been absolved. If the princess was more than alright with her not being her true love, whether or not someone else could be shouldn't matter at all.

And yet, the princess is clearly more angry than she'd been before. Except this time she's not upset about her own fate, she's upset about a part of Sylvie that has absolutely nothing to do with her.

"Why would it have been fine if I just liked men?"

The princess laughs. Sylvie's confusion begins to turn to rage. She's spent all week mentally torturing herself over how upset the princess would be when she found out.

And then she *wasn't*.

Until she was.

"Because some people do, silly," the princess says. "But everyone—"

"How do you know that?" Sylvie pushes herself to her knees. The anger's spread all the way to her waist now.

"What?"

"How do you know they just like men? What if they're just confused too?"

"That's not—" the princess blinks. "That's not the same thing."

"Why not?" Sylvie feels her voice raising and can't be bothered to fix it.

"Everyone knows—"

"Why?" she stops her. "Why is it so believable that other people can like one gender or another or both but not that I like none? Why are they allowed to know themselves and I'm not?"

"Because that's not how it works!"

"You can't possibly—"

"I said that's not how it works!" the princess's eyes widen. She draws a long breath. "I don't want to fight with you Sylvie, okay? Please just... I already said I don't want you to feel like you have to lie to me. Just—"

"Then why are you practically begging me to!"

The princess sighs.

The rage reaches Sylvie's head.

"I don't think you're lying on purpose, Sylvie," she says softly. "I know you probably believe what you're saying, but that doesn't... everyone can fall in love with at least someone." She stands to reach for her. Sylvie jumps away. "It's not... have you ever even heard of anyone who can't? I haven't. They don't exist. It's—"

"You just did." Her shoulders are heaving. She doesn't know why she's suddenly so defensive. She's heard all this before. Just never from anyone she actually cared about.

"Excuse me?"

"You. Just. Did. I'm right here, Princess!" She plants herself directly in front of her. "If you want proof that people like me exist, I'm right fucking—"

The princess moves around her without so much as a glance. Within seconds, she's on the other side of the cell.

"What are you—"

"I need to go," the princess mumbles. "I'm not having this conversation with you if you're going to keep lying to my face."

"Don't you dare—"

"I need to go." She gathers up her blankets and pulls open the door. "There's enough oil to get you through the night. I'll see you tomorrow, if you've calmed down enough by then."

"I'm not the one who—"

She kicks the door shut behind her.

"Princess!" Sylvie screams. There's no response. "Fuck you!" She yells just in case she can still hear her.

Then, she retrieves the abandoned mug from beside her cot, chugs its remaining contents, and chucks it at the door for good measure.

The Last Princess of Rosenly

The last princess of Rosenly is an expert at breaking.

She's broken oaths and promises. A kingdom and her parents' hearts.

Her skin. Her spirit.

Herself, in a million tiny, unperceivable ways.

The last princess of Rosenly has never been anything more than the shards of a broken dream too coveted to throw away and so, since conception, she's left nothing in her wake but bloodied, too-soft fingers.

She falls into her bed, squeezes her blankets around her fists and does her best to fall asleep for an hour; not because she wants to avoid the dungeon, but because she knows she has to.

The last princess of Rosenly is an impossible thing; A *dangerous* thing, concealed beneath powders and fabrics and too-thin skin.

She is also a princess, though, so eventually, she pushes herself out of bed, recollects her blankets, and presses against the slightly discoloured brick on her fireplace.

(All princesses are selfish. It's her birthright)

When she returns to the dungeon, she finds the prisoner curled on her cot, facing the wall. For a moment, the princess thinks she might be asleep. Then, she notices the tray wedged between the bars of the cell's door and realizes she's likely not the only one too wound up for rest.

"Sylvie?" she risks whispering. "I'm—"

The prisoner shifts, but it's only to curl herself further.

The princess sighs. The tray's an ineffective blockade. She could reach through the bars and remove it just as easily as the prisoner could, then unlock the door and be right beside her in seconds. But it's the only blockade the prisoner has, so she doesn't let herself touch it. Instead, she sits down on the wrong side of the cell.

"I'm sorry," she offers, weaving her fingers together. "I know I shouldn't have... I promised not to leave you. Repeated it earlier tonight, actually. Then I... I shouldn't have run away. I'm sorry. I'm really never abandoning you though, okay? Sometimes I'm just... temporarily stupid. I'm sorry."

"You apologize," the prisoner grumbles. "For a princess."

She frowns, trying to make sense of it. "You mean too much?" she guesses.

"Not nearly enough. Still more than you're probably supposed to, though."

The last princess of Rosenly risks leaning forward slightly. "Does that mean—"

"That was what, thirty minutes?"

"An hour," she corrects.

The prisoner snorts. "I'm not pissed you left for an hour. I'm pissed about all the shit you said before that."

The princess's shoulders deflate. "I know. I shouldn't have—"

"I've felt terrible," the prisoner tells the wall. "I've been *destroying* myself over letting you think I could save you, and you didn't even care about that! You tried to fucking comfort me over that! Only to turn around and treat me like some kind of abomination just because—"

"You called me that," the princess remembers. "An abomination. Not that—"

"You're not supposed to exist!" The prisoner exhales.

"I already apologized for that," she mutters. "Or... I said that because what you are caused real, tangible harm. That doesn't mean it's your fault, but it's at least a reason to be mad. If you were pissed I couldn't save you, that'd be fine. But you *weren't.*" She crosses her arms over her chest. "You didn't freak out because something about me was hurting you, you started screaming at me because apparently you're so incapable of believing that I know more about how I work than you do that something that has absolutely no impact on you made you—"

"I believe you!" the princess blurts. "I'm…" She licks her lips. "I do. That wasn't… I'm sorry. I do."

Slowly, the prisoner rolls over. "Then why the fuck—"

"Because I *can't* believe you." Her chest is suddenly heaving. She presses a fist against it, but it doesn't slow. "I'm…" she tears at her lip. "I believe you, I know you're right, I just… I couldn't. I can't. I'm… if you're right, that's… if that's possible, I'm…" She feels a single tear slip down her cheek and bats at it. She won't let herself cry. She's the one who keeps doing everything wrong tonight. She doesn't get to cry about it.

Masking her emotions is the only regal training the last princess of Rosenly has ever excelled at, but something about being alone in the darkness—alone in the darkness with *her*—always seems to eat through all her defenses.

"I'm sorry," she whispers. "I'm not… I'm just trying to—could you just try and kill me again so I can stop being the one who has to feel like shit? I'm not… that was a joke. I'm not good at jokes. I don't know why…"

A meal tray smacks against her foot. She looks up. The prisoner holds her eye for a moment before nodding once and returning to her cot.

The last princess of Rosenly wipes at her face. "Does that um… am I allowed to come in again?"

The prisoner shrugs. "'s your dungeon."

"Well, yes, but I don't want that to make you feel like you have to—"

"Stars, Princess. Yes, okay? Can't try to kill you when you're all the way over there."

She scrambles for her keys. The princess lets herself into the cell then hovers in place, unsure of what to do next.

"I'm sorry," she repeats, since that's at least true. "I shouldn't have made that about you. I'm—that *wasn't* about you. I—I think it's wonderful you… it's too wonderful. I'm… I just couldn't think about how wonderful…"

(Princesses who fantasize about never falling in love do not get to see adulthood)

"I'm sorry," she's suddenly crying. She's weak. She's pathetic. She's incapable of not making everything about herself.

(All princesses are selfish. It's her birthright)

The prisoner opens her arms to her. "Come."

She shakes her head. "I'm… I can't. Thank you, I mean, but even knowing you don't want any of… that. From me. I still can't—"

"Come hug me instead then. If you want."

She frowns. "But you're… you're mad at me."

"Yeah. Turns out you tricked me into caring about you at some point," the prisoner smiles slightly. "Fucking bitch. Come here," she nods. "It's okay."

Instead, she falls. "It's not fair!"

"I know," the prisoner moves closer. "It's not. None of it is."

"The stars didn't even give me a fair chance! They… you talk about them like they're good! How can this be—"

"Just because you haven't fallen for anyone yet, doesn't mean—"

"Yes," she whispers. "Please. Don't. I'm sorry, I… don't."

"Okay." The prisoner scoots even closer. Her knee's practically touching the princess's, but it isn't. The last princess of Rosenly knows she won't let it.

So, she lets herself throw her arms around her. "I'm sorry," she says.

"I know."

"I'm sorry!"

"I know."

"I'm—"

"Stop it, Princess. I… forgive you?"

The last princess of Rosenly freezes. She pulls away. "You do?" she watches her carefully.

(Princesses worthy of saving rarely get to stop anything at all)

"I do," the prisoner nods.

"I'm grateful, it's just… you don't sound sure."

The prisoner snorts. "Yeah, I… that's kind of new for me too, actually." She leans forward. "I do, though. I promise. I get… why you'd react like that."

"Thank you," she whispers.

"How long have you suspected?"

"Since I was ten?" she pretends to guess. The last princess of Rosenly remembers the exact moment it first occurred to her. An incurable curse is not the kind of thing one easily forgets. "I… we started with men. Boys, actually. They were… my parents didn't go through all that to not have a blood heir, so we started with princes from other kingdoms then lesser nobles then… when we ran out of children of any sex my age in Rosenly and knew we'd have to widen our scope, they asked about preferences to try and make things more efficient and I realized for the first time that other people have those? And that mine was to be with no one at all? What about you?"

"I think I just always knew," the prisoner shrugs. "Pretty sure I was just made that way. You had a lot more reasons to hate the idea of that than most other ten-year-olds, though, so maybe—"

"Does it matter?" she interrupts. "If I was born destined to never fall in love with anyone or grew into it? Either way, it's not… it scares me, Sylvie. I don't just not feel it, the thought of someone else… that's terrifying to me. That's always going to be terrifying to me."

The prisoner doesn't respond.

"Do you… sometimes I think I might have been made as some kind of punishment. A child who needs true love's kiss to survive who's physically incapable of experiencing it. Because the stars were angry they were forced to grant a wish. Do you think—"

"No."

"But maybe—"

The prisoner puts her hand beside hers. The last princess of Rosenly doesn't let herself take it. She doesn't deserve it. Not yet. Not tonight. "If you were built to punish, they wouldn't have made you so… you."

The princess swallows. "I hurt you tonight," she whispers. "Twice."

"Yeah. Most people can't. Most people aren't worth giving a shit over. I'm…" the prisoner watches her. "If I had to fall in love with someone, I wouldn't hate it if it was you."

"But you won't."

"I won't," the prisoner nods.

She grins, then realizes what she's doing. "I didn't—" the princess blushes. "I just… you're the first friend I've had in… you're my first friend, actually. Ever, I think. Even though I know you don't have much of a choice in that and I know a dungeon's hardly—"

"Stop forcing me to admit I like you," the prisoner says. "It's gross."

She smiles openly this time. "You're too important to me to be my true love, I think. I wouldn't have been able to cope with being terrified of you."

"Well then," the prisoner says. "I promise I'll never find you pretty or alluring or even the slightest bit attractive."

The princess nearly cries. "Thank you," she whispers.

"I'll kiss you if you want me to, Princess," the prisoner says. "But I don't think I'm ever going to be able to beg, okay? You need to be the one to ask. I need to know it won't destroy you."

She should do it right there and then. She should get it over with as quickly as possible. The princess's eyes find the abandoned box she forgot in the cell. "Are you still awake enough to lose a few more card games?"

"Hey! That's not—" the prisoner allows her to change the topic.

The last princess of Rosenly raises an eyebrow.

"Okay, fine," she grumbles. "But you could at least pretend to be less cocky about it."

"You don't actually want me to do that."

"No," the prisoner smiles. "I don't."

Sylvie

"Sylvie, Sylvie, Sylvie!"

The princess has started becoming more and more reckless with her arrivals to the dungeon. Now, she announces them well before pushing open the hidden door.

Sylvie doesn't mind. If anything, it gives her a few moments to find something to busy herself with so they can both keep pretending her life doesn't stop every time the princess leaves her. This time, she pretends to be in the middle of the book stashed beneath her cot. The princess is quicker than usual, though. And earlier. Sylvie's not sure if she catches a glimpse of the tallies she's been scratching into the underside of her mattress before she shoves it back down.

When the door opens, the princess looks even more disheveled than usual. Her hair seems to grow thinner with every passing day, but usually, it's at least combed. It's brighter outside than it typically is when she arrives, but instead of the underskirts—or occasional fully intact gowns— she typically visits in, she's in a light cotton shirt and brown slacks.

Sylvie doesn't have to pretend to drop the book. "What—"

The princess lowers the tray in her hands enough for Sylvie to read her expression. She's smiling. It's maniacal and far wider than usual, but if anything, that's even more of a comfort. The princess's forged expressions never get to be this big.

"It's been pouring all day," the princess explains, propping the tray against her waist and fishing through her pocket for the key. Once she's found it, she leaves the cell door wide open for at least half a minute as she sets down the tray and puts on the lamp. Sylvie can't get her eyes to leave it.

The princess would be a terrible warden if Sylvie was anything but a model prisoner, and Sylvie's never been a model anything.

But she doesn't want to go. She is a girl born for the skies who's spent weeks away from them, but there's nothing waiting for her out there. Here, there is a princess with a penchant for tears and a maniacal smile. She'll go when they come for her, of course—if they're still coming—but for now, this is the only place Sylvie knows how to be.

"They cancelled everything," the princess continues, finally remembering the door. She doesn't appear the slightest bit panicked as she moves to close it, though. It's almost casual. "Normally they wouldn't, but *someone* tried to kill me a few weeks ago, so we're taking security a lot more seriously." She sits down beside the tray and waits for Sylvie to join her. "Thanks for that, by the way." She points at her with the spoon.

Sylvie rolls her eyes. "I really don't think you understand how you're supposed to react to assassination attempts, Princess."

"I never have."

She nudges the tray towards Sylvie. A guard just left with her dinner, but on it sits a bowl of some kind of thick, orange soup. "I spent the day helping the staff," she says. "It was really more observing than helping, obviously. They wouldn't let me do much. But it still felt like finally *doing* something, you know? I feel like I haven't gotten to actually do anything in ages." She winces, catching herself. "Sorry, I didn't mean to... I'm sure you'll do plenty of useful and even more useless things after they let you go."

"We could leave right now and get a head start," she says. The princess's eyes instantly move to the mattress. She's seen it, then. Sylvie doesn't let her gaze follow. "Bet there's less guards out there with all the rain."

"*Sylvie.*"

She forces herself to smile. They're both running out of time. "I'm gonna keep trying."

"I know. So," the princess claps her hands against her knees, changing the topic. "Anyway. I had the day off, so—"

"So you spent it with the kitchen staff?" It's just supposed to push her back on track. It's not supposed to come out as defensive as it does.

"Are you jealous?"

"No," Sylvie grumbles.

The corners of the princess's lips curl. "Did you... want to spend more time with me?"

"Absolutely not!"

The princess laughs. "You're my *friend*, Sylvie Castell. You like being—"

"I'll dump that entire bowl all over your stupid clean shirt."

She just keeps laughing.

"Stop—"

"You don't need to be jealous," the princess whispers, leaning forward. "I almost came first thing this morning. My mother knew I would and was waiting right there to stop me. I wasn't allowed to come until the guards finished for the day."

"Oh," Sylvie says. "Well it sounds like *you're* the one who likes being around me then, actually, so—"

"Yes, Sylvie. Most of us are fine just admitting that." She nudges the bowl. "I made this. All by myself."

"Most people can make soup, Princess."

"Just try it!"

Sylvie does. Then, she immediately spits it directly back onto the tray. "Skies and—" she can't even get through the exclamation; even speaking somehow hurts. Her entire face feels like it's burning, every hair follicle practically vibrating in pain. It won't be herself or the dark that finally destroys her once and for all, then, it'll be a skyscorned bowl of soup.

She's dimly aware of the princess giggling, but she holds up a hand to try and block it out. She can't focus on anything but the lack of feeling in her tongue right now. She's very seriously considering scraping it along the dusty floor to at least introduce a better taste.

"Sylvie," the princess is laughing so severely that it takes her a moment to get the word out. "Here. No need to be so dramatic."

Sylvie has several colourful responses in mind for that, but her mouth isn't cooperating well enough to voice any of them. She accepts the mug of water the princess is dangling in front of her face and downs the entire thing in a matter of seconds. When she looks up again, the princess is still laughing.

Sylvie glares. "You're a monster."

"You tried to kill me!"

"Which was *far* more humane!"

The princess pulls the cot closer then lies down against it. She doesn't flip it over, but Sylvie still knows. She saw the tallies. It'll only be a matter of time before she brings them up. "I really did try to make it edible," she explains. "And the kitchen staff tried *so hard* to pretend it was. Which I enjoyed far more than I should have, I think. It's probably a good thing I won't live long enough to rule. I would've gone mad with the power."

Sylvie stiffens. From anyone else she'd expect a reminder of imminent death to be some kind of guilt tactic, but the princess is as blasé about hers as most people would be about the weather. Sylvie isn't, though. It hits her in the gut every time she mentions it, each strike worsening a bruise that long ago became unbearable. But the princess is casual and light and something akin to happy, so Sylvie has to be too.

"You rushed all the way down here to give me the worst soup ever made," she says.

"Yes," the princess nods proudly. "I made them save it just for you. I considered asking them to send it down with supper without an explanation, but—"

"You realized that'd be a cruel and unusual punishment?"

The princess sits back up just to smirk at her. "I realized I wouldn't get to watch." She falls back onto the cot, wildly gesturing with her left arm until Sylvie gets the hint and lies down beside her. "I love rain, I think," she whispers. "If it rained every day for the rest of my life, I still don't think I'd ever tire of it."

"Weather wishes are some of the easiest, you know," Sylvie says. "The stars almost always—"

"Stop trying, Sylvie."

"That wasn't even an escape attempt," she says. "I just..." she sighs. "You've seemed happier lately, okay? If a little bit of rain would help with that, you could sneak me out for a few minutes once it's darker, we'll make a single wish, then sneak back in and blame it on a gardener or something, okay?"

The princess is quiet for so long that Sylvie begins to hope she might actually be considering it, but then she just says, "you really care a lot about making me happy, huh?"

And Sylvie says, "I'll end you."

The princess laughs, rolling over to face her. "It's not just the rain," she admits, tracing a wrinkle in the cot. "It's... I'm not happy I'm dying, but I've spent seventeen years and

Nonymous

ten and a half months doing it. I've gotten used to it. And it's not… I thought it was my fault. For all seventeen years and ten and a half months. That I wasn't good enough or trying hard enough or that I didn't want it badly enough or… when everyone tells you that falling in love is supposed to be the most important, most natural thing you'll ever do and you put in that much time and effort and it doesn't work, you start to feel like you're broken, a little. But now I know. You're like me. There are other people like me. And I'm still dying, but now at least for a month and a half, it feels like that's less my fault."

Sylvie swallows. "None of this was ever your fault, Princess."

The princess just nods.

"You can tell your parents," she suggests. "That you know it'll never work. Then you won't have to wait for rain to take a break. You can spend these last few weeks—"

"I'm not breaking their hearts over a month ahead of schedule, Sylvie," she stops her.

"Your heart matters too."

"My heart only exists because they needed it to. I'll be fine. I have you to distract me. And dozens of games left to beat you at."

Sylvie rolls her eyes. Then, now that her face isn't burning with jealousy or spice, she processes. "I never told you my last name, did I? You said it earlier."

The princess's eyes widen. "I didn't mean to… my parents, um, mentioned it. They're slightly concerned with how much time I'm still spending down here and thought… I'm sorry. I didn't want to look into you without asking first."

She forces her expression to remain calm. Sylvie needs somewhere for her energy to go, though, so she sits up.

The princess follows.

119

"You found something, then. Something worth not mentioning."

The princess looks away. "I didn't—"

"You wouldn't be apologizing if you hadn't found something."

She chews at her lip. A drop of blood slips down to her chin.

Sylvie sighs. "It's okay, Princess," she says. "Not your fault. Whatever you found or that you found it. You can ask about it."

"You should hate me," she whispers.

And Sylvie instantly knows exactly what she's found. Her heart hammers. She presses her fingers against the ground to try and reallocate her blood. "It wasn't your fault," she reminds them both. She won't let herself take it out on her. Not again.

(She can never help herself)

"But if I hadn't—"

"It's not your fault," Sylvie repeats. "Did they tell you why they took him? Or make up some BS to make themselves sound more justified."

"They said he was weaving," she said. "A star went up right above your house, so it was easy to—"

"It was for my little brother," she keeps her tone and sightline even. These are just facts. She can recount facts. "He broke his arm the week before and we thought it'd be fine, but then all at once he started to get really sick and then he kept getting sicker and—he shouldn't have done it." She feels her whole body shaking. She can't let them be anything more than facts. "We could've borrowed a cart and ridden to the nearest healer. He probably would've been fine if we had. It was reckless and stupid to turn to the stars without even *at least* leaving the house first, but...he was being stupid and he got caught. That's it."

"It's not stupid to want to help someone, Sylvie," the princess says softly. As she leans forward, she doesn't take Sylvie's hand, but she does link one of her fingers through hers. "That was—I didn't know it was to heal someone. It wouldn't have been right to lock anyone away for any kind of weaving, but I didn't—he was helping his *child*, Sylvie. You don't stop and think through every possible consequence when someone's in trouble like that, you just act."

It's simple. It's so, so simple coming from her lips. But it's the first time Sylvie's ever properly heard it. Immediately, she falls apart.

"I'm sorry," the princess says. "I shouldn't have... I should've just let you talk. I should have—"

"Thank you," she whispers.

The princess hesitates for a moment before enveloping her in a hug. She smells like soap and spice and as Sylvie breathes her in, she tries to summon enough excitement into her chest to convince herself that she might actually be able to save her, but all she feels is calm.

"Did they..." the princess eventually risks asking. "They said they let him go, but that's... that's why you're a part of whatever you're a part of, right? For revenge? Because he... he wasn't okay, was he?"

"No," Sylvie whispers.

The princess holds her tighter. "Was he... after that happens to a weaver, do they ever..."

"I don't know." She pulls away to wipe at her face. She's crying, somehow. That's new. "They umm... my mother thought it'd be better to get him under stars—any stars—once we had him back. They left. Them and my brother—Bash, that was his name—they... I don't know how it worked."

"You didn't go?"

"I needed to stand by our stars."

"They let you?"

"I was fourteen. We were already used to staying with other constellation members during the night. They thought I was old enough to be on my own."

"You weren't."

Simple truths, it turns out, can destroy a person far more rapidly than complex ones.

"No," Sylvie whispers. "No, I wasn't. I'm still..." she sniffles. "I wasn't."

"I'm sorry."

Sylvie shakes her head. "You didn't know."

"I do now." This time, the princess puts her entire hand over hers. "You don't belong on your own, Sylvie, alright? I'm not letting that happen."

"Yeah," she nods at the bars. "You've made that very clear."

"That's not—"

"I know," she stops her. "Thank you."

The princess squeezes her fingers. "I'll keep coming back to annoy you until the very end, okay?" she whispers. "I'm never leaving you."

Sylvie forces herself to smile through the new wound. At least when the princess leaves her, it won't be because she's choosing to.

It'll just be because Sylvie wasn't enough.

(She can never help herself)

The Last Princess of Rosenly

The prisoner is waiting for her to die.

The last princess of Rosenly has no right to feel as hurt by that as she does.

The prisoner is a prisoner. She's been trapped in a cell for almost a month. It's only natural that she's eager to escape it.

But she's also the last princess of Rosenly's friend. The only one she's ever had. And she's counting down to the day she'll die.

She does her best to forget the tallies on the mattress

(a dying princess does not have time to be a confrontational princess, after all)

but she can't. Every time they laugh together, every time they cry together, it's all she can think of.

And the prisoner notices. It only takes the princess a few days of trying not to stare at it for the prisoner to march straight over to the mattress, flip it over herself, and hurl it at the princess's feet. Twenty-four thin lines sliced into the top layer of fabric. They stare at each other in the aftermath.

"I'm a prisoner, Princess," the prisoner breaks the stalemate. "I can barely see the sun. You don't get to blame me for wanting to know how long it's been."

"That's not—"

"We can pretend to be happy, carefree equals as much as you want, but I'm still your prisoner and I'm still allowed to—"

"You're not supposed to want me to die!" she breaks.

The prisoner falls silent.

"Twenty-eight days," she continues. "If you wanted to know how much longer you'd have to wait, I could've told you. I could've told you any point of any day because I'm thinking about it constantly but you—you're supposed to pretend you're not looking forward to it! You weren't supposed to let me know you were adding up how much longer you'd have to wait."

The prisoner reaches out an arm as if to touch her then thinks better of it. "That's not what that's for. That's... I don't have anything else waiting for me after this, Princess. You know that. Why would I be—"

"Why else! You're not tracking the days for the sake of it, you're hiding it because you knew it'd upset me. You're—"

"I'm hiding it because I can't talk to you about why I need to know how long it's been."

The princess deflates. She crumples to the floor as her anger leaves her, replaced only with the melancholic calmness of defeat.

Slowly, the prisoner crouches down beside her. "I think we should leave, Princess," she says. "Soon."

"You claim you're not counting down to me dying one second then try to get me to help you escape the—"

"Listen to me!"

The prisoner sounds just desperate enough that she does. When she looks up, the prisoner's staring straight at her.

"I don't want to escape," she says slowly. "Don't get me wrong, I did, but now I don't... I'd rather not be in a cell, but I don't have a single person waiting for me out there. I can wait a few more weeks. I don't want to escape."

"But you keep—"

"But I keep bringing it up," the princess says slowly, eye contact unrelenting. "Because I think we should *leave*," she repeats. "Soon."

The princess frowns, realization setting in. "But you said... you said it wasn't bad. What they—"

"You're going to think it's bad," she whispers. "I'm sorry, I didn't…you're going to think it's really, really bad."

The last princess of Rosenly flies to her feet. "Then tell me how to stop it!"

The prisoner winces. "I can't… I can't. I'm sorry."

The princess breathes so frantically it physically pains her. She made herself let it go.

(Princesses worthy of saving rarely get to stop anything at all)

She *knew* there was something coming, but she let it go because she was pathetic enough to pretend that didn't matter. She'd been desperate enough for someone to like her to accept her own undoing.

And the prisoner had said it would be okay. The girl who had held a knife to her throat, who was depending on the princess for absolutely everything, who had freshly experienced the terror of what might happen if the princess decided to hate her had said it would be okay.

And she'd *believed* that.

(Princesses worthy of saving rarely get to stop anything at all)

She's suddenly too dizzy to be sitting, but instead of lying down, she straightens her spine. She will not allow the prisoner to see how deeply she's weakened her.

"I'd already said I wouldn't let you get hurt," she attempts to keep her voice low and even, but even she isn't a good enough actress to keep it from shaking with rage.

"I know."

"I'd *promised* I wouldn't abandon you."

"I know, I—"

"You didn't have to lie! I was so careful to make sure you didn't feel like you'd have to—"

"I wasn't lying, Princess!"

She leans forward. "Tell me what's coming." She hates the way her voice sounds. Loathes that she can't stop her eyes from watering. "*Please,* Sylvie. Just—"

"I can't," the prisoner looks away. "It's not... people could get hurt."

"So you'd let them hurt me instead?"

The prisoner hisses. She turns away from her. She's a coward. "It's... complicated."

"It *shouldn't be*," the last princess of Rosenly realizes. "You said there's no one there for you! You... I've protected you. I care about you. They sent you here. They knew it would destroy you and they'd still—"

"I had starlight," the prisoner mumbles. "A bit of it. In a bottle. It..."

"Would that have even worked?"

The prisoner doesn't respond.

She scoffs. "They are the kind of people who'd send you here to suffer on their behalf. I'm—"

"Stop it." The prisoner's shoulders lock. She's hit a nerve. Good.

"No one out there gives a shit about you!" she pushes. "I do! You tried to kill me, and I still do! You can't—"

"Stop it, Princess." When the prisoner turns, her eyes are dark with rage. The princess makes herself hold them.

"No!" she says. "No! That doesn't make any sense! Why are you protecting people who've clearly never cared about you when—"

"You don't even have a name!"

The princess freezes.

"You wanna talk about people not giving a shit about you?" The prisoner stands. As she does, she looks taller, somehow. Anger's added a few inches. "No one even bothered to give you a fucking name."

"That's not…I have one. It's just… when it took too long to anchor myself, my parents changed their—"

"Yeah? What do they call you now then, huh?"

"I don't—"

"Get up," the prisoner says.

"What?"

"Get the fuck up."

The princess does. She doesn't know why, but she does.

(Princesses worthy of saving rarely get to stop anything at all)

"You mean so little to them that they haven't bothered calling you anything for almost a decade." The prisoner presses a single finger against her chest. It burns her.

"My parents brought an entire kingdom together because—"

"Your parents *forced* an entire kingdom to do their bidding because they knew they wouldn't be able to love a child that wasn't theirs! And then they got you and you did such a terrible job being their child that they couldn't love you either!"

She stumbles back. "Sylvie, stop."

(Princesses worthy of saving rarely get to stop anything at all)

"You don't call them anything either, you know," Sylvie accuses. "It's just 'parents'. It's always 'my parents'. Tell me something about them. Tell me a single thing about either of them that differentiates them from the other."

(Her mother looks at her even more sparingly than her father does)

"You can't!" Sylvie meets her silence. "You can't because they don't give a shit about you. They're probably *actually* counting down the days until—"

"They're not."

"Sure," Sylvie snorts. She takes a step back, but even in her absence, the princess finds she can't move at all. "You don't get to pretend to know who does and doesn't care about me, Princess. Not when you're so pathetic that you couldn't get a single person in an entire kingdom to love you."

The last princess of Rosenly squeezes her eyes shut. She knows if she doesn't, the prisoner will get to see her cry. When she's finally collected herself well enough to open them again, the naive part of her is secretly hoping to find an apology or remorse or even just a seed of regret,

(Hope is a very hard thing to kill in a princess, after all)

but the prisoner's still exactly where she left her: breathing. Glaring.

She stumbles to the door, fumbles with her key, and lets herself out of the cell.

The prisoner laughs. "Running away already?"

"No." She smooths out her pile of blankets. "I said I'd stay. I'm staying."

"I don't want you to!"

The last princess of Rosenly takes a deep breath. She straightens her spine. Fixes her smile. "I know."

Neither of them speak at all for the rest of the night. The last princess of Rosenly isn't certain she remembers how to.

Sylvie

Sylvie Castell will never get any wishes, but if she had one, she'd wish to stop being so fucking reactive.

She's unsure what that would even look like—maybe the stars descending to sever her tongue whenever she's about to say something she'll regret—but that hardly matters. This is why she was supposed to let herself be destroyed from the inside out that first night.

A Sylvie who can think is a Sylvie who can react. And A Sylvie who can react *will* hurt. Sylvie has never done anything that didn't inevitably hurt someone.

(She can never help herself)

She wasn't oblivious to the princess's anger. If it wasn't initially justified—and she's still not certain it wasn't—it was at least recognizable. Sylvie is no stranger to feeling like anger is the only defense you have left. She'd almost considered just letting her yell. It had felt easier than continuing to talk about all the reasons she couldn't warn her about what was coming.

(And far safer than confronting how desperately she wanted to)

But then the princess had gotten too close to the truth and Sylvie had destroyed things.

(She can never help herself)

She should have apologized. She'd had ample time to apologize. But it had felt too much like confirming that the princess was right.

She *will* apologize tonight, though. They don't have time to waste on anger and the princess has a far larger right to it. Sylvie'll force herself too, even if it destroys her.

She isn't the one falling apart.

The hidden door begins to move again less than an hour after breakfast. It's sunny out. She's been staring at the window ever since the princess left, so she knows it's sunny out and there's absolutely no reason for it to be her, but hope and excitement propel her to her feet regardless.

Confidently, impossibly, the King of Rosenly enters the dungeon. Sylvie feels her knees begin to buckle but luckily, she's close enough to the bars to catch herself against them. "What happened?"

The King and Queen of Rosenly have been diligently avoiding her cell. Even with the tunnel, they don't allow their daughter to visit under anything but the cover of night. But he's here. And the princess isn't. Something's gone terribly, horribly wrong.

The king doesn't respond. He just watches her. His expression is unreadable.

"I'm a weaver," she searches for reasons he might have come to her. "I'm... if something's happened I could—if anything's wrong, I wouldn't hesitate to—I'd help. Let me help."

She's giving too much away, but none of that matters. Something's happened. The last thing she did was scream at her. She needs to fix it.

For once, she needs to fix something.

Slowly, the King moves to the wall. He leans against it. "I hear my daughter's been spending a lot of time down here." His voice is low, but not as low as she'd thought it would be. Sylvie realizes abruptly that she's never heard him speak.

"She's... yes. So if something—"

"I assume she's told you, then? That she begged for your release?"

"No," Sylvie says. "I didn't—"

He holds up a palm, silencing her. "My daughter's not as good a liar as she thinks she is. Neither are you. I'm sure I don't need to tell you how easy she is to manipulate."

"That's not…" Sylvie tries to calm herself down. A father would not speak so negatively about his child if something disastrous had happened. She hopes. "I'm not… we're friends." She's never heard a word sound so pathetic. It's not enough. It's not what they're supposed to be.

(Sylvie doesn't get to save her)

"I'm supposed to believe that?"

"You never do anything you're supposed to do," Sylvie says. "Doesn't mean it's not true. If she's in trouble—"

"She is."

She feels her breath stop.

"She thinks she's befriended a prisoner who refuses to even try to kiss her."

The princess is alright. The princess is still alive enough for Sylvie to be a problem.

Sylvie crosses her arms over her chest. "She doesn't want me to."

"That's not what she said when her mother found her in her room sobbing this morning."

Sylvie stills. It's a lie. She *knows* the princess would tell her if she was ready. She just isn't sure if it's a lie the king invented, or one the princess fed him. "I'll kiss her when I'm ready to," she decides. "She knows that."

The king sighs. "She's a fragile thing, Sylvya. Luckily for you, she's fragile enough to beg for the release of the girl who tried to kill her. But you won't be able to keep convincing her you're worth saving if you wait too long."

"That's not—"

"I think it'd be in everyone's best interest if we finally learned the truth, don't you?"

Sylvie swallows back a rebuttal. If the princess is lying, they can just lie some more. Refusing to ask the princess to kiss her clearly isn't what's won her her safety. If the princess still isn't ready, they'll just lie and say they tried and failed. "Okay," she whispers. "I'll… we'll try. Tonight."

The king smiles. "Good."

Sylvie almost lets herself relax when he reapproaches the tunnel, but then he emerges with a single lit torch. She frowns. "What are—"

Without so much as looking at her, he scoops up one of the blankets the princess keeps just inside the cell, approaches the window, and stuffs it in front of it. Sylvie leaps to her feet. "You can't—she'll hate you!" she threatens. "She'll realize what you did and… she'll hate you!"

The king doesn't so much as flinch. Keeping his back to her, he turns, walks back to the door, and closes it.

He takes the light with him.

The Last Princess of Rosenly

The last princess of Rosenly is going to say she forgives her.

(Princesses worthy of saving don't get to hold grudges)

She doesn't, but how she actually feels rarely matters. She's running out of time. If whatever the prisoner's counting down to truly is as awful as she's made it sound, she might have even less time left than she'd previously thought. She doesn't have time for grudges.

(That doesn't mean she doesn't wish she did)

"Hello." When she enters the dungeon, the prisoner's already ignoring her. She's entirely still, sitting cross-legged on her cot and pointedly facing the wall. The princess sighs, putting on the lamp before extinguishing her torch. "You're not being fair, Sylvie," she says. "I shouldn't have to... I'm allowed to fight to protect myself. You told me I was in danger. I wanted to know how. There was nothing wrong with that."

The prisoner doesn't so much as twitch.

She sighs, fiddling with the key. "I'm sorry though, okay? If I took things too far. I didn't... I wish I could figure out how to protect myself without hurting you."

She enters the cell. The prisoner doesn't acknowledge her.

"Sylvie. I said I was sorry."

She doesn't move.

"You're unbelievable!" She marches towards her. "You—I'm going to be dead in a few weeks and you—"

The moment the princess touches her shoulder, the prisoner whips around. Something's *wrong*. The last princess of Rosenly knows it immediately.

The prisoner's eyes are red and bloodshot, the skin around them slightly bruised, as if she's been pressing against them for hours. They don't focus on the princess, even when she's right in front of her. The pieces of hair framing her face are tangled beyond salvation, a few clumps of black still clutched in her shaking fists.

The last princess of Rosenly freezes. "What—"

Sylvie practically snarls as she pounces on her.

"Sylvie!" She tries to push her away, but it's useless. Sylvie might've spent a month in a cell, but she hasn't spent years dying. The princess's body was not built for combat. "What are—"

There are hands on her back. There are hands on her back and they're coarse and rough and pulling.

"Stop it!" She doubles her efforts, but she can't break free. "I said I was sorry! You can't—"

One hand snakes higher. Past her shoulder blades. The back of her neck. It finally slows to press against her hair and the princess freezes.

This is not how this happens.

This was inevitable, but it's not supposed to be how it happens.

"Stop it!" She tries to swat at Sylvie's arms, but it does nothing. Sylvie's practically staring right through her. "You can't—not yet, Sylvie. You can't—you can't! You—"

She manages to back up slightly, but Sylvie follows. There's only so far she can go before running into the wall and then, she's even more trapped.

The last princess of Rosenly knows she's supposed to close her eyes and let it happen. It's inevitable, after all. This won't be her first time, and it won't be her last. She's supposed to be numb already. She shouldn't be this scared.

But this is *Sylvie*. Sylvie who screamed and clawed and tore her to shreds last night, but still Sylvie. She doesn't know how to exist in a world where Sylvie's done this.

Sylvie leans forward. The prisoner's head makes contact with stone. There's nowhere else to go. There's nothing she can do. She shakes her head anyway.

"Please," she whispers. She has both palms pressed against Sylvie's chest, but it won't be enough. She can already feel her forearms shaking. "I don't—you can't.... You can't! *Please*." She feels herself start to cry. She feels her elbows bend. She gives in and squeezes her eyes shut.

(This is her favourite part of kissing, of course: getting to finally close her eyes)

Sylvie

Sylvie returns to the present with disgust, horror, and a single gasp. She's not sure where she's returning from. She's not certain she was ever gone at all. All she knows is that suddenly, she's in a cell, pinning a sobbing princess to the wall.

The princess hears her breathing change and shivers, pushing her chin towards the ceiling to try and claim at least the illusion of space.

From her.

From Sylvie.

"No." She pushes herself back so rapidly that she leaves a layer of skin against the stone. "I didn't... *no*."

It's not until she speaks that she processes the ringing in her ears, but she forces herself to ignore it. Nothing else can matter right now.

The princess doesn't open her eyes once she's released her. She just cowers and shakes and shivers. Sylvie's mind's still too scattered to make sense of, but she's certain of at least one thing: she's a monster.

(She can never help herself)

It only took a little bit of darkness to turn her into one.

(Maybe she has been all along)

She rises on shaking legs and risks taking a step toward the princess, but she must hear the movement, because she immediately flinches. Sylvie takes a step back. "I'm not going to hurt you, Princess." Her throat aches and her head is far, far too loud, but she needs to make herself talk. She needs to *fix it*.

(For once, she needs to fix something)

"I swear, okay?" she continues. "I'd never—"

The princess's entire body jolts.

Sylvie swallows. She drags herself to the opposite wall and tries to support herself against it. Her body is screaming at her. It's desperate to curl up and disappear.

But first, she needs to fix it.

(For once, she needs to fix something)

"Walk out of the cell, Princess," she whispers, both to soothe her throat and because she's terrified anything louder will shatter them both. "Close the door. Lock it. Go all the way back to your room, if you have to."

The princess doesn't move. Sylvie's not sure she's able to.

"Okay." She squeezes her eyes shut to try and clear her head. It doesn't work. "Pass me the key?"

She's not expecting that to work either, but inexplicably, without so much as looking up, the princess slides it towards her.

"Okay." Dizziness overwhelms her as she bends to retrieve it, but she forces herself back up. Slowly, she backs out of the cell and closes and locks it behind her. It's the first time she's been out of it for weeks, but she doesn't have the mental capacity to process that yet. "I'm tossing you the keys," she narrates, terrified the sound might make things worse. "The cell's locked. I'm not... I'm *never* going to so much as touch you, but even if I wanted to, no one can get to you until you choose to come out, okay?" Finally, she gives in to her aching limbs and collapses beneath the lamp. "You're alright," she tries to reassure them both. "You're okay. You're.... I'm sorry. I'm so, so sorry." Her voice and chest shake. She buries her face in her knees just in time to stop herself from sobbing openly. "I'm so sorry!"

For a long while, there's nothing in the dungeon but the flickering of lamp light, the sound of breathing, and the shaking bodies of two broken girls. And then, eventually, one risks opening her eyes.

"There's a guard in the tunnel," the princess's voice is so quiet she almost misses it.

Sylvie looks up.

"If…" The princess shakes too severely to support herself as she tries to stand. "There's a guard in the tunnel. If you try to run, there'll be…"

"There's not," Sylvie says. "But that's okay. I already knew that. I'm not going anywhere, okay? You can lock me right back up as soon as you're ready to."

"N—" This time she makes it to her feet, but instead of moving forward, she stumbles back. "No. There's a guard. There's—"

Sylvie stands to unhook the cuffs hanging beside the lamp. "Do you have the key to these?"

"You can't—"

"Princess," she tries again. "Do you have the key?"

She nods.

"Okay." Sylvie latches one end around her wrist. Her fingers shake as she does. She tries to ignore that. "Okay." She closes the other around one of the bars. "I'm not going anywhere until you let me." She tugs at the chain to demonstrate. "Take your time. It's okay. You're okay."

The princess collapses back against the wall. "Why did you…" she starts. She draws a deep breath. "Was it because of yesterday? Was it—"

"No!" she panics. "Of course not! Stars, Princess, I—" She sighs. She shouldn't have placed the cuff so high. She's unused to being this aware of how heavily her skin sits on her bones. "I was an asshole yesterday, okay? I didn't mean to… I was going to apologize. I should've apologized right away. I'm sorry."

"But you attacked me."

She winces. "That wasn't... I don't know what that was," she admits. "It... I was terrified and confused and I think because it was the last thing we talked about I genuinely thought kissing you was the only way to... I thought you wanted to. I'm sorry. He said you wanted to and I *knew* that was wrong, but I don't..." She tries to remember any of the past several hours. She can't. "I got confused, at some point. And I was too... It's like I'm everywhere at once, I think? Here and not? But I'm completely here now, and I'm not letting myself anywhere *near* you, okay? You're safe. Next time I get lost in the dark, you don't come close until you're sure I'm here. Not that I'm expecting you to come back," she realizes. "If... if you don't feel safe ever coming back, if this isn't the kind of thing you can move past, that's completely..."

"The window's covered," the princess whispers.

"Yeah," Sylvie nods. "Yeah, I... your father came to visit. He was worried about you." She's not convinced he was, but it feels an important lie to offer after everything she said yesterday.

"How long?"

"What?"

"How long did he leave you like that?"

"I don't..." She squeezes her eyes shut again. "I'm not sure. I don't remember. But no matter how long it was, you don't have to—"

"Are you okay?"

She could almost cry. "It's not your job to ask me that, Princess," she whispers instead. "Not after what I just—not after *anything* I've done to you."

The princess looks away. "I didn't know," she says. "That he'd try to hurt you."

139

"Of course you didn't."

"It's my fault, then. I shouldn't have… I let them see me cry. I wanted to prove to myself—"

"Don't you dare try to make this your fault," Sylvie stops her. She winces against the pain in her head but pushes forward regardless. "You have nothing to feel guilty about. You take as long as you need to hate me. Forever, if you want."

"You didn't hurt me, Sylvie," the princess argues, because of course she does. "Not really. You—"

"Yes," she looks right at her. It makes her vision blur. "I did."

The princess nods slightly before standing back up. "I thought you'd run," she says, taking a hesitant step towards the cell door. "I thought… you've been bringing up escape constantly, so when I realized I'd handed you the key, I… Why didn't you run?"

"You know I haven't seriously been considering escaping for ages now."

The princess frowns. Because of course she doesn't. The one time Sylvie actually told her the truth, she immediately followed it up by attacking her. "You keep bringing it up. It's all you care about. It's—"

"No, Princess, I care about you. It's…" She digs her toe into the dirt. "It's always been because I cared about you. That was the one thing I got right yesterday."

The princess doesn't respond.

"I'm going to tell you, okay?" she decides. "I can't not… You were right. I should've told you yesterday."

"Because my father tortured you."

"Because you *deserved to know*. Because you're the only thing in this whole entire kingdom I wouldn't be able to live with myself if I didn't protect, okay?" She swallows. "I can't... Not everything. Not anything specific enough to get anyone in trouble. But I'll tell you everything I can, okay? When we're both a bit less terrified. If you still want me to."

The princess nods. "Sylvie?" she says.

"Yes?"

"You're shaking. And bleeding."

She grimaces. "I'll be fine."

The princess scratches at her arm. "And you keep staring at my starlight."

She instantly averts her gaze. "I'm sorry."

"Not at me, just the light," she continues. "I know the difference, you know. Is that... You're still shaking. You sound like you've already spent hours screaming."

"None of that's your problem."

"I think it is, though," she whispers. "I think you are."

Fingers wrap around hers. Sylvie risks looking up, but only long enough to confirm that the princess is now right in front of her. She can't risk staring again. It'll terrify her.

"Is it because it'll help? Last time it seemed like... and you said starlight's better than other light sources, right? Does it help?"

She wants to pull away, but she can't get her fingers to uncurl. "I'm not going to touch you," she whispers.

"Like this is okay." The princess keeps their fingers intertwined as she opens the door and unlocks the cuff. "If it helps. As long as... Just hands though, okay?"

When Sylvie's legs inevitably buckle, she's already there to catch her. Sylvie quickly pushes herself away. "You can stay outside the cell the entire time tonight," she reiterates. "Or go back to your room. Or every night. You—"

"Does it help, Sylvie?"

"You shouldn't be trying to help me! I just—It makes no sense to—"

"It makes no sense that you didn't just run. I think that's… It's what happens when you care about someone, isn't it? You do things that shouldn't make sense."

"Not if it hurts you," Sylvie shakes her head. "Not after I've hurt you."

"I believe you didn't want to, though."

"That shouldn't matter!" she explodes.

The princess jolts.

"Shit, sorry," she buries her face in her hands. "Sorry, I—"

"Sylvie," the princess gently tugs at her arm. Once again, her fingers find hers. "Does it help?"

"I don't deserve…"

"And I don't deserve to be dying," the princess stops her. "And Rosenly doesn't deserve to suffer for it. And you didn't deserve to get hurt and I didn't deserve to get attacked. But I do deserve a best friend functional enough to remember me once I'm gone, so I'm asking one last time, okay? Does it help?"

Sylvie licks her lips. She can't even look at her. "It does," she whispers.

"Alright then," the princess squeezes her fingers. "Then I'm staying right here."

The Last Princess of Rosenly

The thing in her chest isn't fear.

It's fast and frantic and just beneath bearable, but she knows it isn't fear. Because instead of quickening when it presses against Sylvie's pulse, hers calms. It's easier, she thinks, that Sylvie was so clearly not herself. There is a Sylvie who attacked her and a Sylvie who didn't and for now, at least, she's strong enough to carry them separately.

She leads Sylvie into the cell by the hand. It feels ridiculous to stop and lock the door now that they've both been on the other side of it, but she does anyway.

(Her mind will never stop telling her this is all a trick)

The thing in her chest isn't fear, but she knows whatever's in Sylvie's is. Even enclosed within hers, her fingers still shake. Her eyes refuse to stop moving. Her every breath is audible.

This girl was just tortured. This girl was just tortured *because of her*.

(She'll never know how many people were tortured in this dungeon because of her)

"You can still go," Sylvie continues to insist as she coaxes her down onto the cot. The princess desperately wants to offer her water, but she's scared of what she might return to if she leaves. "If you change your mind at any point."

"I won't."

"I attacked you," Sylvie says. "I *terrified* you."

The princess considers, running her tongue along her gums. "That was... I've kissed thousands of people, Sylvie. I've hated it in a different way each and every time. I've never reacted like that."

The other girl flinches. "I know. That's why... I tried to physically force you to—"

143

She smiles weakly. "You're far from the first person to do that."

"I hurt you, then! You did everything you could to get me to stop and I still—"

"Not the first to do that either," she stops her. "Please don't pretend to think you were."

Sylvie falls silent.

"I think…" she takes a deep breath. "It was because it was you, I think. I think… I really don't want to kiss you," she whispers. "Not just… partially because then I can't keep pretending it might work, but also… I like being around you, Sylvie. I really, really like being around you, most of the time. And once it happens… I don't want my every interaction with you to be tinged with the taste of your tongue in my mouth, okay? If you want to apologize, let me stay. Don't make me sit in the memory of tonight. I don't want it to be what sticks."

"'s your dungeon," Sylvie mumbles. "If you want to stay, you can—"

"Let me stay, Sylvie. Be nice to me. I'm… I can't handle anything sharper tonight."

"Okay," she lets her eyes fall shut for a moment, leaning back against the wall. "Stay. Please." Slowly, she raises one eyelid. "No promises on the nice thing, though. Still not very good at that. But I can be not-mean."

The princess grins. Then, she stares at their interlocked hands. "It would've always helped, right? Touching me? Or… The starlight, but also… Even when you're not like this?"

Sylvie looks away. "I didn't want to scare you."

"I know." She pats her knee. "That's why you never tried to touch me unless I wanted you to. I think… I forgive you, Sylvie. If you need me too. Because that so, so obviously wasn't you, okay? So just… be my friend again? Please?"

She feels her try to pull away, but it's weak. Feeble. "You shouldn't—"

"I don't have time for grudges," she stops her. "And I already spend the rest of my day listening to constant apologies. Don't waste my nights on them too."

"But—"

(Princesses worthy of saving rarely get to stop anything at all)

She shifts to face her better, pressing a finger against her chest. "I am in charge of what I do and don't forgive. Stop trying to take that from me."

Finally, Sylvie nods. "Okay," she whispers. "Thank you."

"I'm supposed to apologize too," she says. "Now that you can actually process what I'm saying properly, right? For hurting your feelings yesterday?"

Sylvie rolls her eyes. "You absolutely shouldn't apologize for that. I was just being a wuss."

"Good," she nods. "I'm glad we agree."

"Can we just…" Sylvie yawns. "I know you're running out of time, but maybe call it a night early? 's not like… I can't do much thinking right now. Or talking. But tomorrow—"

"Okay." The last princess of Rosenly slowly releases her fingers and gets up to retrieve her blankets. She considers dramatically grinding the one over the window beneath her heel until it comes apart, but decides against it. It's just another blanket. Maybe they both need it to just be another blanket.

Instead of setting up beneath the lamp like she usually does, the last princess of Rosenly brings her pile back into the cell.

"What are—" Sylvie starts.

"You can't even breathe properly," the princess explains. "You're not going to be able to sleep without me. Just my hand, though," she quickly adds. "Not because I don't trust you specifically, I just—"

"Princess. You don't need to justify things when you're already doing more than you should."

"Right." She pushes her blankets closer to the cot and attempts to get comfortable before holding out her arm. "Good night, Sylvie."

She's expecting her to echo the sentiment, but Sylvie croaks, "I was wrong, yesterday."

"We can talk more tomorrow. It's okay. You already—"

"You're not the pathetic one," she pushes through. "I've had seventeen years to try and get an entire community to care about me and was just enough of a disaster to fuck up with every single person there. But you…" She pauses to cough. "I'm the first person you've had enough time to let properly get to know you in years, Princess," she says. "Maybe ever. And I'm clearly awful with people and knew there wasn't even a chance I'd be at all romantically attracted to…" She pauses again to clear her throat. The princess really should have insisted on getting her water. "to you and I came here specifically to hold a knife to your throat, but I'm physically incapable of not giving a shit about you. You're so easy to care about that it's wildly inconvenient sometimes. That's… I think you're kind of amazing, actually."

The princess smiles. Her chest is simultaneously light and aching. "Thank—"

"I'm only being sweet because I'm tired," Sylvie stops her. "I'll deny saying any of that in the morning."

The princess snorts. "Good night to you too."

Sylvie

The princess arrives the next day bearing tea, ointment, and bandages.

"Hey," she smiles, carefully kicking the door closed behind her. "Are you... feeling any better today?"

"I'm not going to touch you," she says instantly.

The princess shakes her head. "Not what I was worried about." She slips the tray through the bars to free up her hands to unlock it.

"The umm... window stayed uncovered all day," Sylvie says. Her voice still shakes, but only slightly. She's going to be fine.

(She's not sure she deserves to be fine)

"That's good." The princess sits and gestures for her to join her.

Sylvie does. Of course she does.

(She can never help herself)

"You don't have to worry about that, okay? I talked to my parents. That's never happening again."

"The guard who came with lunch also checked the oil," she nods towards the light. "It's been on all day."

"Oh," the princess says. She picks up a bandage. 'Let me see your knees. I can—"

"Why was it on all day?"

"Oh." The princess chews at her lip. "I umm... It should've been. The moment I saw how bad it could get that first time I was late, I should've... We're a castle, we've plenty of wicks and oil. I think the only reason I didn't bother anyone about it sooner might've been to give myself an excuse to keep coming down. Which is ridiculous because putting on a lamp never actually justified spending the whole night down here, but..." she trails off. "Knee, please."

Sylvie hisses when she makes contact.

The princess smiles slightly. "Baby."

"I am not! Anyone would—"

The princess's eyes flick up to hers. Sylvie sighs.

"Most people would react. 's not my fault you're inordinately tough."

"Sure." The princess continues to dab at her skin until she's removed enough grime and gravel to bandage it. "Thank you, Princess," she mutters before moving on to the other leg.

Sylvie rolls her eyes. "Thank you. For the light too. I umm…" she searches for something to offer. "You never need an excuse to come. I like it when you're here. Kind of."

"I know," the princess nods. "My starlight works even better, right?"

She frowns. "That's not… I like having to tolerate you. You specifically, not just the starlight."

When the princess starts to grin, she instantly realizes she's fallen into a trap.

"Stars, Princess!" she kicks at her. Only at her, of course. She's not sure she'll ever let herself touch the princess again. "You're such a bitch!"

"It's not my fault you're only nice to me when I make you feel guilty enough first!" she laughs.

"I take it back. Completely intolerable. Worst person I've ever—"

The princess presses the teacup into her hands. She takes a sip.

"Thanks. Worst person I've ever met."

The princess keeps laughing. "Drink all of it," she instructs. "It's good for sore throats."

"Yeah. Believe it or not, I know how tea works."

"It's the best one for sore throats, actually," the princess corrects. "I've caught virtually every illness imaginable. Trust me, I'm probably the best expert in the kingdom."

Sylvie frowns. "You say a lot of really disturbing shit way too casually you know."

She nods. "Thank you."

Sylvie knows what she's supposed to do next, so instead of doing it, she takes another sip of tea. Then she waits to finish the entire cup before setting it down. "I said I'd tell you things yesterday."

"Oh, right," the princess says. "I forgot."

"No, you didn't."

The princess chews at her lip. "I'm supposed to say you didn't have to mean that. Since you said it under duress. And I'm supposed to be trying to not exploit the power I have over you."

Sylvie arches an eyebrow. "Are you gonna say I didn't have to mean it, then?"

She looks away.

Sylvie rolls her eyes. "It's okay, Princess. Very normal thing to want answers about." She sighs. "If it makes you feel any better, I didn't change my mind because I was upset or scared or... whatever I was." She risks looking right at her, but she can only hold it for a moment. "You were really, really scared. And I obviously knew I didn't *want* you to be scared, but seeing it... I don't think I can cope with not warning you."

The princess waits.

Sylvie waits.

The princess leans forward. "You still haven't told me, Sylvie," she whispers.

"You can't tell your parents," she says. "I know that's not fair, but you can't... they might not even go through with it. It might not even work. I can't tell you the specific date and time, but I swear on anything you want me to that if it comes, I *will* make sure you have time to get out in time, okay? But if you act early... fuck!" She rakes her fingers through her hair. "Fuck, this... I can't do this! I can't—"

"You said you needed to."

"That's the whole problem!" Sylvie takes a deep breath. She's not ready for the secret she's meant to be sharing, so she reaches for another one instead. "You still haven't figured it out, have you? What you actually saw in my eyes?"

The princess frowns. "I don't... no. I made a mistake. You were there and you were my age and I was desperate to play pretend, so I—"

"You recognized me, Princess."

She waits for clarity to set in, but it doesn't. The princess just keeps frowning at her.

Sylvie sighs. "You don't remember."

"You said you'd never lined up before. You—"

"You were eight," Sylvie stops her. "I was nine. Your parents had just finished throwing their first temper tantrum about how weavers 'weren't doing enough' to get the stars to make you fully human. They'd just started restricting weaving and—"

"I was kidnapped," the princess gasps.

Sylvie nods. "You remember?"

She shakes her head. It doesn't make any sense. Sylvie's spent every day since thinking about that night. She ruined a kingdom for a girl who doesn't even remember she existed.

"Okay, then," she tries to appear unbothered. "We took you. The adults thought they might have more luck using wishers who weren't your parents, but your parents refused to see reason. They figured best case scenario, they'd fix—not fix," she stops herself. "That... sorry. Bad word."

"Cure," the princess supplies.

She shakes her head. "That's not... change," she decided. "Anchor. They thought either they'd anchor you and your parents would be overjoyed and come to their senses, or they wouldn't and nothing would change because your parents clearly already were intent on fully banning weaving altogether soon. We had you for a few days at most. You were... small. Scared. Didn't talk at all, just cried all the time. They kept you in my room because we were about the same age and they figured it would... it didn't. You wouldn't talk to me either." She picks the cup back up. She's unsure why, it's been empty for a while. She puts it back down. "You were just so... loud. And sad. And scared. And..."

"And the stars didn't actually miraculously listen to me, did they?" the princess finishes for her.

Sylvie straightens. "I never once tried to use that to manipulate you," she says. "I might've pretended not to know why you thought you felt something when you first saw me, but I never let myself pretend the stars might actually—"

"Sylvie." A gentle palm presses against her knee. She looks up to meet kind, light-ringed eyes. "I know," the princess says. "It's okay."

"It makes sense you wouldn't remember," Sylvie continues, flexing her fingers. "It's easier to compel the stars with some kind of ritual, but it's not always needed. You were wishing so desperately and it was so bright and long and it was practically touching the sky already so I..." she swallows. "It took less than half a thought. Then the stars started to swirl and there wasn't time to do anything but get you to an empty field so no one would be held personally responsible and there were enough stars then that they at least couldn't trace it back to which house it originated in, but everyone knew. They had you and I ruined it and made everything worse and no weaver could ever so much as get close to you without several escorts ever again and it was all my... I did that. That was my fault. So I can't... I want to tell you everything," she admits. "I want—whenever I let myself make my own decision, it ends terribly! I can't—I won't ruin everything again! It... I'll tell you what I can, because I know you deserve to know. But not everything. I can't let myself tell you everything. But I swear if you agree you'd hate it and want to run, you'll have enough of a warning to do that."

The princess is quiet. "I wouldn't consider letting me go ruining everything. Just... if you were wondering."

She shakes her head. "They would've though. If I'd just let myself wait a few more days or maybe it would've actually worked and they wouldn't have to..." she sighs. "I'm not stupid. I know if it didn't work your parents still would've been pissed and were always inevitably going to ban weaving altogether, but it might have taken more time. If they'd been able to deliver you back to them safe and cared for and claim good intentions instead of letting them think we were planning on holding you forever."

The princess scratches at her arm. "Is that what they're planning, then? To take me again? To try and see if—"

Sylvie must wince visibly, because the princess stops herself mid-sentence.

"It's worse," she whispers. "Isn't it?"

Sylvie shakes her head. "It depends on..." she stops too. She's done with lying to herself. "Yeah. I think you'll think it's worse."

The princess scoots back to lean against the wall. Sylvie follows.

"Tell me," she whispers.

She feels like she's supposed to be holding her hand or arm or at least *something*, but Sylvie doesn't let herself. "I can't tell you when or how," she starts slowly. "I can't tell you how I'm involved—beyond saying I'm not going to hurt you, Princess. You have no reason to fear me—but they think if they can get you alone and get enough weavers together, they might be able to get it to pause."

"The deadline?"

She winces again. She should be being more direct, but she can't make herself. "No, it... you. Your parents think it's some kind of trick, of course, so they'd need to... they practiced. On rabbits and squirrels and eventually even a human volunteer or two. They said it feels like falling asleep, Princess, except it makes everything stop. You don't get older, your starlight doesn't get burnt up, you're just... paused."

"Why?" The princess doesn't look horrified yet. Sylvie's still skirting around the truth.

"Your parents claim they'll repeal all anti-weaving laws the moment you..."

"Die," the princess supplies.

"Die," Sylvie nods. "But they won't. You must know they won't. They promised not to take out their frustrations on us if you didn't end up anchoring yourself, and you saw what... it's always been grief driving them, even when you still had a decade left. If you actually die, it's going to get worse."

"I hardly think they'd perfect it if I just spent an eternity stuck in some kind of—"

"It's so they wouldn't have to stop the lines, Princess," she forces out.

The princess is silent.

"They'd… they could make it mandatory for everyone who crosses into Rosenly to try. They could add decades to the deadline, so long as they agree to encourage weaving again. Wishes stick better when the stars start off closer. It'd be easier to maintain with more in the sky. Then, once the right person kisses you, we'd just—"

"There is no right person, Sylvie." She stares right at her. "There's never going to be."

"I know, but—"

"Do I get a say?" she demands. "If they take me, if I say I *don't want that*, don't I—"

She can't respond, so she shakes her head instead. "Fuck!" The princess punches the floor. "They can't—fuck!"

"I'm sorry," Sylvie slowly rises to her feet. "I know—" she reaches out to grab her forearm when her fist starts to fly again, but the princess tears herself away.

"Don't fucking touch me."

Sylvie nods. She backs up. "I'm sorry," she repeats.

Then, she says nothing else at all. There's nothing she can say. She knew the princess would be horrified, but she knows no way to fix it.

She sits, she watches her self-destruct, and she waits.

The Last Princess of Rosenly

They're going to turn the last princess of Rosenly's body into a tourist attraction.

(Princesses should be ogled and not heard)

They want to trap her alongside the stars beneath her skin. They want to keep her corpse warm enough to be used for centuries.

(A corpse cannot cringe at a stranger's spit)

And it would fix things. The worst part is how instantly she realizes that it would fix things. Her parents are flawed and selfish and rule Rosenly off of their whims and their whims alone, but those include their want for a child.

A frozen, eternal child with no need to parent is their every dream come true. They would hand the kingdom directly over to the weavers if that's what it cost to keep her that way.

The last princess of Rosenly's failure to find her true love has condemned hundreds of her people. Her failure to die will save them.

But she *doesn't want it.*

(She'll have to learn to)

(Princesses worthy of saving sacrifice everything)

(Princesses worthy of saving rarely get to stop anything at all)

She screams and kicks and hits, not because she knows she won't be able to avoid her fate, but because she knows she's not allowed to.

(Princesses worthy of saving rarely get to stop anything at all)

Once she's exhausted enough to stop, she stumbles onto the cot, pulls her knees to her chest, and allows herself to go numb.

155

(Princesses worthy of saving rarely get to stop anything at all)

"Here," Sylvie eventually appears across from her, holding out her palms. She nods towards her busted knuckles. "Let me fix it."

She shakes her head. She'll need to let her eventually. She was already selfish enough to get Sylvie hurt once; she can't go back upstairs with unexplainable injuries.

But for now, she needs to feel normal.

"Later," she says. "I can't... I need to—"

Sylvie gets up to retrieve the ointment and bandages. "This okay for now?"

The princess nods. She holds out her still-shaking fists. Sylvie's fingers are lighter than the wind, so fast and fleeting as they move against her skin that they barely feel like they're making contact.

The last princess of Rosenly knows that's for her own benefit. She knows she's supposed to be terrified now that Sylvie's admitted that the comfort all weavers covet most lies just beneath her skin. But she isn't. She craves a pressure that demands nothing from her at all.

Sylvie will never be able to give her that—no weaver will—but she at least wants to pretend.

(Hope is a very hard thing to kill in a princess, after all)

But Sylvie's touch is light and her fingers are fast and she can do nothing to change any of that because she doesn't know how to articulate the distinction between a touch that comforts and a touch that burns. Maybe there isn't a distinction at all.

Sylvie dabs at a particularly large cut just above her ring finger and the princess pretends to hiss in pain. Finally, Sylvie's hands slow slightly.

"Are you… pretending to wince to make me feel better?"

"Oh, no," she says. "That was me making fun of you."

Sylvie laughs. It's rough and low and almost solid enough to press against her skin. Almost. "You're such a bitch" she mutters, half to herself, half to the princess.

She smiles. "I'll have to wish them better before I go," she admits as Sylvie moves to start wrapping her knuckles. "There's really no point treating them."

Sylvie continues to wrap the bandage. She lets her. "Sometimes," she says as she secures it. "It's more about knowing someone cares enough to want you to be okay than the actual getting okay part." She never looks right at the princess when she's being sweet, so when Sylvie looks up again, the last princess of Rosenly already knows she's about to say something stupid. "Plus I'm a bit squeamish. For an assassin."

"You weren't when you were bleeding yesterday."

Sylvie looks away again. The princess is fairly certain she catches the faintest hint of a blush as she does. "Maybe I'm just squeamish about you, then. I don't know." She pushes herself to her feet. "What are we doing now, then? What new game have you brought just to brag about how—"

"Sylvie." She catches her hand. "You won't tell me when they're going to try and take me?"

Sylvie sighs. "If it seems like it's actually happening, I'll warn you in time, okay? But I told you, I can't—"

"It's soon though, right? It's… I'm running out of time. It would have to be."

She doesn't respond.

"And you're… you being here is part of it?"

She looks away.

"Do you think I should just let them take me?" she whispers. "You kept saying I should run, but if they think that might work, do you think I should…"

"That's not my decision to make."

She chews at her lip. "I can't not, right?" she says. "Rosenly's supposed to be my kingdom. I'm supposed to protect it, not… not cause all the hurt I've already caused. If I'm the only one who'd have to suffer and I probably wouldn't even feel it, then I have to—"

"Okay, changed my mind," Sylvie drops back to her knees. "My decision now. You're going to do whatever you need to do, okay? Not what you think your kingdom needs, not what you think anyone else wants, whatever's least likely to destroy you."

"But shouldn't I—"

"Nope," Sylvie shakes her head. "Too late. My decision. It's your potential eternity. You're doing whatever you're going to be able to live with."

"Or die with, actually."

"See!" Sylvie exclaims. "That's extremely casually disturbing!"

The princess is supposed to smile at that, but she can't. "I think I want you to kiss me now."

Sylvie frowns. She instantly shifts to cross her legs and sit more properly. "No," she says slowly. "you don't."

"I need you to, though," she amends. "I need… I'll have to eventually and until then I'll have to keep worrying about it and—"

"You literally just said you're terrified of kissing me!" she says. "Me specifically! More than you've ever been of anyone else."

She nods. "That's why we have to, though. I can't keep being terrified."

And, if it works, she won't have to make a decision at all.

(Hope is a very hard thing to kill in a princess, after all)

Sylvie sighs. "We could just never try. I know it's not going to work and you know it's not going to work, so—"

"What if it does?"

Her entire expression falls. "Oh, Princess," she whispers.

"I don't think it will," she quickly explains. "I'm… it's not because I'm feeling… things. For you. I still don't think I could. But I need to be certain. It'll keep driving me mad until I'm certain."

Sylvie rests her forehead against her palms and closes her eyes.

The princess waits in strained silence.

"Can we wait a day?" she asks. "Get a little more distant from me trying to assault you then check in and see if you still want to try?"

She considers. She pretends to consider. She's desperate to procrastinate. "Okay," she whispers. "That would… that works."

"And then," Sylvie says. "Tomorrow, if you still want to try, we do everything we can to keep it from being a terrible memory, okay? What's your favourite dessert?"

The princess frowns, confused. "I… chocolate covered strawberries?"

"Good. You use your disgusting amounts of wealth and power to demand a plateful, okay? You bring that and your favourite game and literally anything else you can possibly think of that makes you happy, we spend two seconds on the kissing part, then, whether or not it works, we spend the rest of the night eating your favourite food and doing all your favourite things, okay? Make the kissing the least memorable part."

The last princess of Rosenly smiles.

(She could almost cry)

"You're using me to get fancy castle desserts," she whispers.

"Oh, I'm absolutely using you to get fancy castle desserts. I also…" She looks away again, so the princess knows something achingly honest will follow. "You said it might ruin us. Doing… this. That's not… I'm good at ruining things. Too good at ruining things, actually. But ruining this would be… let's not, okay? Let's try to make it less than terrible."

"Okay," the last princess of Rosenly says. She wants to promise her that it won't ruin anything at all, but she's already spent far too much of her life lying to appease others.

The Last Princess of Rosenly

The last princess of Rosenly is not naive enough to mistake the swirling in her stomach for anticipation, but as she makes her way through the tunnels, she tells herself that's what it is anyway because it's easier to cope with.

She has no real reason to be this nervous. It's hardly her first kiss; she's kissed dozens of strangers in the past few hours alone. And this is Sylvie, who started soothing her tears long before she'd given her any reason to and whose touch is so gentle it aches. She knows it will not be bad.

But this is *Sylvie,* who started soothing her tears long before she'd given her any reason to and whose touch is so gentle it aches, so she knows it will be horrible.

When she pushes open the door to the dungeon, Sylvie's lying on her cot. The princess allows the door to slam shut out of habit and winces as Sylvie jolts into consciousness.

"Sorry," she whispers, slipping the tray through the bars to free up her hands for the key. "Were you... asleep? If you're tired, I can—"

"'m fine," Sylvie sits up. "Figured I might be up later than usual tonight, so... not that we have to be," she quickly adds. "Completely up to you. I just wanted to make sure I wasn't too tired to stay up if you needed me to."

She's already been planning out how make things easier for the princess. That should calm her.

It doesn't.

She enters the cell. She picks up the tray.

"You brought the strawberries."

"I did," she's abruptly breathless. "I had to request them first thing in the morning so they'd have time to harden. I'm pretty sure the kitchen staff was wildly annoyed by the whole thing but I'm dying, so…" She doesn't know what to do with her hands once the tray's no longer in them. She gestures nonsensically as she crosses her legs to sit down.

"You're scared," Sylvie says.

She can't help but laugh. "I'm terrified."

"We don't have to—"

"I do, though," she says. "If you're okay with it." She realizes all at once that she's never made sure she's okay with it. "Are you?" she panics. "We don't have to, if—"

"I'm fine, Princess."

"But you also don't… you're like me," she remembers. "You're like me. You don't want to either. I shouldn't have just assumed that the moment I was ready—"

"I don't really care about kissing," Sylvie stops her. "Tried it once or twice. Didn't hate it, but I don't get why it's such a big deal either."

She hates how jealous she gets at that. How unfair it is that the thing that's defined her entire existence can mean nothing at all to someone. "But you're… like me."

(Unless she's not)

(Unless she was lying)

"Guess we're different on that part," Sylvie shrugs. "Kissing's just… a thing people do. For me. Like holding someone's hand or giving them a hug."

"You don't hate it?"

"I don't hate it."

She genuinely does care about Sylvie. It's not right that she's so upset she doesn't hate it.

"Which means," Sylvie shifts positions to kneel on the cot. "I'm super unimportant here, okay? You decide when. You decide how. You even tell me how to stand and the exact number of seconds we try it for if that'd help, okay?"

She considers. "I don't want to make you do anything you wouldn't want to," she whispers.

"You won't," Sylvie says instantly. "Biggest thing I'm worried about doing is scaring you. I trust you."

"But—"

"Completely, Princess. More than anyone. I trust you."

She takes a deep breath. She tries to smile. "Does that mean you finally respect me enough to start calling me Your Highness?"

"Fuck no," Sylvie says. "Means I respect you way too much for that."

This time when she laughs, it's almost real. She crashes into the silence that follows far too quickly. "Strella," she decides.

"What?"

"It's…" She's suddenly embarrassed. She should not be this embarrassed by a name. "Strella. If you wanted to call me something. That's… I think I would like it if you gave enough of a shit about me to call me a name."

Sylvie smiles. "Okay, Estrella."

"Just Strella!" she quickly corrects. "That one's not… we're not supposed to use that one. My parents… they're still my parents. I wouldn't want to use something that I know would hurt them. Even if they don't hear it."

"So you're going with… practically the exact same name? That I'm almost certain also means star?"

She feels her face heat. "Okay so maybe I also got a bit too used to the original one, okay?" she mutters. "I'm not that creative. I don't keep track of many names. Just… Strella feels less like direct disobedience."

"Alright. Fair. Tell me exactly how you want this to go then, Strella."

She hands her a strawberry. "First, we eat. You've been eating dungeon food for a month, I'd rather you taste like chocolate. No offense."

Sylvie snorts. "Insult me as much as you want if it gets me fancy castle chocolates." She accepts the strawberry and takes a bite. Her eyes widen. "Skies!" she gasps, already reaching for another. "These are actually good?"

"You didn't think they'd be?"

"You're a princess! It's not my fault I assumed you had terrible taste." She eats the second berry right to the leaves then licks chocolate off her fingers.

The princess stares at them.

"Sorry," Sylvie smiles sheepishly. "Look, here." She wipes her hands off on her pants. "No one's getting touched by any mouth goop."

She frowns. "Beyond the goop in your mouth?"

"Right," Sylvie nods. "Shit, sorry. Just... alright. Dessert eaten. What next?"

She unlatches the chessboard. "We play. We get to the move before I win, then—"

"What if I win?"

She stares at her.

Sylvie scowls. "You're kinda mean for a princess, you know that, Strella?"

She beams. "Yes," she nods. "Correct. We get to the move before I win, pause, do it then, then finish the game. That way, I have something to look forward to."

"And after?"

"After?"

"What do... if it works or if it doesn't, is there anything—"

"Stop touching me either way," she decides instantly. "Move as far away as you can, actually. Not because I'm worried I'll hurt you or that you'll do something to hurt me, I just… I'd need to be alone. No matter what."

Sylvie nods. "Got it."

"And you can't let me win on purpose just to make things go faster. That wouldn't feel as good."

Sylvie rolls her eyes. "Trust me, Prin—Strella," she says. "If there's even a chance I might beat you, I'm taking it."

She sets up the pieces.

They begin to play.

Sylvie

Sylvie isn't going to point out that the princess keeps passing up opportunities to win.

Partially because she's desperate enough to finally beat her that she almost manages to convince herself her first few mistakes are genuine, but mostly because she's terrified by how obviously terrified she is. But then Strella's hands eventually start shaking too severely to place the pieces properly, and she's forced to acknowledge that they can't keep pretending.

"If you don't want to—"

"Stop saying that!" Strella stares at her. Her chest heaves. She forces her hands beneath her thighs. "Sorry," she whispers. "Sorry, it's just... I do. I do. I just... we should. Now."

"You didn't win yet."

Strella sighs, pushing the board away. "You're so terrible it's getting too hard to keep figuring out how not to."

"Hey!" Sylvie takes another strawberry. She nudges the plate towards the princess. "How are we doing this? Sitting or standing?"

"Sitting," she decides. "That'd probably be better."

Sylvie nods. She backs up on the cot, leaving her legs parted to make sure she'll have room.

Strella hesitates. "You can't... don't touch near my ribs," she says. "Sometimes... it feels like they're trying to break me, when they do that. Like at any moment their fingers will slip right through then tear me apart from the inside out."

"Okay," Sylvie nods again.

"My lower body either, actually," she continues. "I'm pretty sure I might only think I'm more okay with that because there's usually too many skirts in the way to feel

166

much but... not there either. Maybe I should've... I should've worn more. I should've—"

"You can go change," Sylvie reminds her. "We have time."

She shakes her head. "I wouldn't trust myself to come back," she whispers.

Sylvie considers. "Stay." She points at the cot. She shimmies around her to retrieve some of the blankets from the corner. She drapes a few over her shoulders. "There." She tries to smile. "No body at all. Easy."

The princess doesn't smile back.

She holds out her palms. "Where do they go, Strella?" she prompts. "It doesn't have to be anywhere at all, but—"

The princess's fingers are already wrapped around hers. She carefully positions one hand against her jaw, pauses to consider, then keeps the other clasped between them. "I think I want to know where it is," she says. "Not that—I trust you. Not that I don't trust you, but—"

"Okay. Makes sense."

Strella draws a long, rattling breath. "I should've done this right away," she says. "Before I cared. I thought it might fix it if it was with someone who cared but... this is worse. This is a lot worse."

"We could—"

Her attention sharpens. "Stop it."

Sylvie nods. It's just about the only gesture she's not worried will hurt her.

"I'm just..." Strella takes another breath. "I don't like how much this feels like some kind of conclusion," she whispers. "I don't want to... even if it works—which it won't. Don't worry, I know it probably won't—that doesn't change anything. Or it changes everything, obviously, but with us, that doesn't… I'm not going to suddenly like you like that just because the stars say I'm supposed to."

"Ditto."

The princess looks right at her. There are already tears clinging to her lashes. "Promise?"

"Of course." Sylvie leans so close that their foreheads are practically touching.

(They're not, of course)

(She wouldn't do that to her)

"Even if every star in every sky and every wisher on earth demanded it of me," she whispers. "I promise I'm never going to find you anything but repulsive."

The princess laughs. It shakes a tear loose and sends it racing down her cheek. "Okay," she says. "Do it now."

"Now?"

"Before I—" She repositions her loose hand and presses it more firmly against her cheek. "I want to feel exactly like this, okay? Hurry up and—"

Sylvie does. She kisses her.

And absolutely nothing happens.

The Last Princess of Rosenly

They never set a time limit on it, but the last princess of Rosenly counts anyway.

One, two, three.

Four, five, six.

It doesn't feel terrible. It doesn't feel good. It is, perhaps, the most average kiss she's ever experienced. When she finally breaks it, she instantly checks her arms

(hope is a very hard thing to kill in a princess, after all)

but the starlight hasn't stilled.

She lets her shoulders relax. Her eyelids fall shut.

And then, she falls onto her side and starts to laugh.

"I'm sorry," Sylvie sounds far away already. She fled to the other side of the cell the moment the kiss broke.

(Sylvie is terrified of touching her)

"I'm so, so—"

She keeps laughing. It's the only thing left to do.

"Princess," Sylvie's already given up on using her name.

(The princess can never hold on to any kind of power for too long)

"You need to try to breathe, okay? Everything's alright. Nothing's really changed. We already knew—"

She's so scared of getting close to her that she slides a half-emptied mug of water along the floor instead of handing it to her directly.

"Strella!"

There are tears streaming down her face so rapidly she can no longer see anything at all. She's not sure how long it's been since she last drew a full breath.

"You need to—"

She must knock the cup over. She feels it seep into her sleeve.

"Stars, Strella. Please just—"

The coldness of the water is enough. She manages one single breath then immediately expels it all to declare, "I'm not contagious!"

"Okay." She hears more than sees Sylvie move closer. "Alright, I know that, okay? Obviously—"

"You won't—" she wheezes. "Touch me. You won't—"

"You told me not to, remember?"

"Well then I've changed my fucking mind!" When firm, rough hands land on her forearm, it takes away the little breath she has left in her chest and forces her into silence. One of the hands moves. A single finger lands just beneath her eye and wipes away the puddle that's accumulated there. She blinks until her vision clears enough to make out Sylvie leaning over her.

The other girl's eyes flick from her left to her right then back again. "Are you okay?"

The answer's too large to explain, so the princess just shakes her head.

Sylvie nods. "Is this?" She squeezes her forearm.

"Yes," the princess whispers. "Please."

Sylvie gently tugs at her arm until they're both sitting up properly then just keeps staring. "Are you…"

The princess pounces at her. She feels Sylvie go entirely still. "Hug me back," she whispers.

"You shook off the blankets," Sylvie says. "Are you sure—"

"Hug me back."

She does. She feels arms wrap around her back. She doesn't imagine bone snapping or ribs separating or skin getting peeled away layer by layer, she simply feels held. And so, she starts to cry.

"Hey." Sylvie's grip loosens, but only for a moment. She slips one hand slightly lower to rub slow, soothing circles against her back. She tucks her chin against her shoulder. "You really need to stop laughing every time your life's on the line, yeah? Makes the rest of us uncomfortable."

The princess laughs. She relishes the way the vibrations in her chest rattle slightly more while pressed against another human being. "I'm so selfish," she whispers.

"Hey, no, you're ridiculously bad at that, actually. For a princess."

She squeezes her eyes shut and allows herself to savour the hug for a few more moments. "I'm *happy*, Sylvie. I'm relieved."

Sylvie pulls away, just like she knew she would. "You're... happy?"

"I know it's terrible," the princess buries her face in her hands. "I know anchoring myself with a weaver—anyone at all, but especially a weaver—would fix everything, but... I didn't know if I was scared because I was worried it wouldn't work or because I was worried it might. Now I know. And I'm relieved. Because I'm selfish."

Sylvie rolls her eyes. "You've spent over a decade wasting almost every second of every day on kissing a bunch of strangers to try and keep the peace, Princess. I'm sure you're entitled to—"

"I'm not," she says. And, "it's Strella. Now."

"Of course," Sylvie nods. "I'm sorry. Strella. Still adapting to that." She sighs, stretching out her shoulders. "I was supposed to let you leave me in the dark, you know," she says. "I'm not good with following plans. I knew if I didn't let my brain break far enough to forget it, I would've inevitably ruined it. Then I asked you to stay. That was selfish."

"That was you being scared."

"Same difference."

"Did they… did they tell you to do that, then? You were supposed to be some kind of sacrifice for something?"

Sylvie shakes her head. "It wasn't officially part of the plan, but we knew it was a risk. It was just one I was willing to take."

"I can't let them take me, Sylvie," she realizes. She doesn't know how she's supposed to trust a group that would allow anyone—allow *Sylvie*—to sacrifice their entire future because of a mistake they made as a child. "Not… I know I should, but—"

"Not if you don't want to."

She licks her lips. "That's selfish."

"Be selfish, then," Sylvie shrugs. "Doesn't sound like being selfless is doing you any better."

She wants to press for more information, but she already knows she won't get any.

Maybe that's the selfishness too. Maybe she's secretly far too content with letting her kingdom burn, so long as it means Sylvie doesn't stop liking her.

"Even if I could stop it, though, even if I stayed here, that wouldn't fix anything either, right? That's… my parents won't stop the line until after I'm gone and it's never going to work, so…"

Sylvie's eyes widen. "You're going to leave."

It's too much, the hope. It threatens to devour her. "I can't," she attempts to quell it. "I could barely… I haven't left the castle since I was eight. I wouldn't even know how to—"

(Princesses worthy of saving rarely get to stop anything at all)

172

"I'd come with you," Sylvie offers instantly.

She smiles sadly. "I'd have to leave Rosenly," she whispers. "They wouldn't be your stars. You said... I'd let you go, I promise. I know they'd blame you if I disappeared. I'd never—"

"Princess." Rough fingers squeeze her smoother ones. "Shit, Strella. Sorry. It's not because I'm trying to be a dick about the name, I just spent a disgusting amount of time thinking about the other one. I'd go." She leans forward. "I'd come."

The princess frowns. "You didn't, though. When your family—"

"And I should've. I'm not messing up again." Sylvie stares straight at her. "I'd leave for you."

She feels it. She forces it away.

(Hope is a very hard thing to kill in a princess, after all)

"We're not soulmates, Sylvie," she reminds them both.

"Fuck soulmates. You've had a shitty decade. I've had a shitty decade. Let's go disappear somewhere and have a less shitty month together, okay?"

She tries to force it away, but she can't. She grins. She throws her arms around Sylvie's neck. "Okay," she whispers. "If...we'll go in two days then, okay? If that's not to—"

"It's not. We have over a week."

"Okay." She says. "What would we need?"

Sylvie considers. "Money," she decides. "Lots of it. Enough to pay people off until we can disguise you. Some kind of portable light source for me if we're planning on leaving during the night—which we should, obviously. Food, maybe? For until we get past Rosenly?"

She nods. "I can do that."

She'll leave a letter too, of course. Her parents would never let her leave if she asked them to, but she at least owes them an explanation. A goodbye.

"If you change your mind…" Sylvie trails off.

She should. She won't. "Don't worry. We're going. I just need time to put things together." She glances towards the door to the cell and licks her lips.

Sylvie gently puts her hand over hers. "I won't be offended if you want to go now, Strella. Or if you've changed your mind and just need space in general."

She shakes her head. "No, that's not… I don't want to be alone, actually. I don't think. Could I…what if I stayed in here the whole night again? Would that be…"

"You're asking for permission to sleep in a cell?"

"Yes?"

Sylvie rolls her eyes. "Be my guest."

Sylvie

She's never been so worried to feel so calm.

Sylvie awakes in the middle of the night not with a gasp, but with a quiet contentment.

It's foreign. It's frightening. She can't remember the last time she felt so completely safe.

She tries to convince herself it's because she's finally close to leaving, but she already knows that's not it. Fleeing a kingdom with its only princess will not be easy. She fell asleep slowly and fitfully.

But now, she's calm. That can only mean one thing.

"Shit," her eyes lock on the window and she bolts up. "*Shit!*"

She longs to savor the sensation, but there's no time. She flies to where Strella's built herself a nest of blankets a few feet away.

"Strella," she shakes her shoulders. "Princess!"

The princess yawns and rolls back over without so much as opening an eye.

"Strella!" she yells. "You need to go. Now."

She flips back over. "What—"

"There are *stars in the sky*."

They both stare. They don't have time to stare.

"I..." Strella slowly sits. "Does that mean—"

"They're coming," she begins to pace. "They're in a line. It has to—"

"They look pretty random. Are you—"

"The *strings* are in a line, Strella!" She knows she has no right to be exasperated. Strella has no way of seeing them. Her fear just needs to be anything other than fear right now. "They're coming. They're on their way. They're probably making wishes as they go to ward off the darkness."

"But you said—"

"Well they clearly lied to me, then!"

(They don't trust her)

(They never did)

(She can never help herself)

(Sylvie doesn't get to save her)

"But—"

"Go!" She shoves her towards the door. She'll let herself regret that later. For now, she just needs to get her to safety.

She's already condemned her own soul. She already decided to prioritize the princess above all else. She will not let her selfishness be in vain.

"But—"

"I doubt anyone's noticed yet," Sylvie realizes. "I think I only did because... it's like everything's different. Warmer, colder, I don't—only weavers would've noticed so you might have enough time to—do you keep any money in your room? Or anything else valuable?"

"I—yes, but—"

"Grab all of it. You need to go. If you don't have time, you just—"

"Are you coming!" the princess interrupts.

"I..." Sylvie frowns. "Yeah. Yeah, sure. Of course. But—"

"You said you were coming," the princess says. "If you're not, I don't think I'd be able to—"

"Skies and stars, Strella, I'm coming, okay? Just—we need to go."

The princess pulls the key from her pocket.

"Okay." She leaves the cell. Sylvie follows.

Strella turns just before pushing open the door. "You wait here, alright? My room's not far. The tunnel's dark. It'd take more time to—"

"Yes, okay," she ushers her into the tunnel. "Just hurry."

Strella hesitates.

(She's going to ruin everything)

"What are—"

"If this doesn't work," she says. "If—"

"If you need to go without me, you go without me."

She frowns. "That's not..." The princess's expression shifts. She takes a deep breath. "Okay." She turns back towards the tunnel. It's dark, black, and infinite. "See you soon."

Sylvie watches her disappear into the darkness, then, she paces the dungeon and waits.

The Last Princess of Rosenly

The last princess of Rosenly hikes up her skirt and runs.

There are bags of gold pieces beneath her mattress. There have been bags of gold pieces beneath her mattress since the day Sylvie held a blade to her throat, but she's been telling herself they're nothing but a precaution. Paranoia. A ridiculous way to quell her racing nerves.

Now, they're her salvation. She grabs a satchel from her closet and stuffs it full of gold, jewelry, and the few blouses and overskirts she can fit. She stops at her desk to scribble a quick note, then throws on a cloak, stuffs a pack of matches in her pocket, and races back through the tunnel.

There's no time to think. There isn't time for anything at all. There needs to be, though. She can't throw away her entire life blindly.

This choice might condemn a kingdom. This choice *will* condemn her.

(Princesses worthy of saving rarely get to stop anything at all)

So, as she runs, she veers to the side. She races into the first room she comes across, pushes open a window, and drops her key ring into the bushes below. She descends the stairs. She continues onwards towards the dungeon.

Sylvie's waiting just beyond the door, but maybe it's for show. Maybe she knows her constellation will arrive any minute and whisk her back to safety. Now that the princess isn't her only means of escaping tonight, maybe she's no longer planning on coming.

It's not that the princess doesn't believe Sylvie cares for her, it's that she does.

It'd be terrible to watch a thing you care about die. Of course Sylvie wouldn't want to be there for that.

So, when she re-enters the dungeon, the princess grabs a lantern from the tunnel and rushes straight to the lamp. She slips the cuffs off the hook beside it as she waits for it to light, using her body to shield it from view. She puts out the lamp.

"Okay," Sylvie says when she returns to her, lantern extended. "Let's—" She reaches out to accept it, and the princess quickly snaps one cuff shut around her wrist. Sylvie freezes. "What—"

The princess closes the other cuff around her own arm, tightening it as far as it'll go. "Let's go," she says.

"What the fuck are you—"

"We need to go."

"No!" Sylvie roots herself in place. "I don't… I'm stronger than you. If I refuse to follow, I could just keep you here until they get here."

She's right. The last princess of Rosenly knows she's right. She stares at her through the flickering lantern light. "Are you going to?"

"I'm…" Sylvie's eyes flick from her to the lantern to the tunnel then back again. "I can't—"

"I'll put out the light if you do!" she blurts.

Sylvie just keeps staring.

"I will!" she insists. "So—"

Racing footfalls sound above them. The princess moves the lantern as far from Sylvie as she can. "Move."

Skies

Sylvie

Sylvie doesn't start running because she believes her, she does it because she can't.

Sylvie Castell has trusted very few people in her life, but as she threatens to plunge her into darkness, Sylvie realizes she let herself trust the princess with every fiber of her being.

Once again, she's become her own undoing.

(She can never help herself)

There's a coldness that follows realizing you would've followed a person into anything at the exact same moment they reveal they've never trusted you at all. A chill that burns to her very marrow. She wants to be mad. She *deserves* to be mad. But if Sylvie stands her ground, she'll be ruining whatever remains of the princess's life.

She should do it anyway. She's supposed to.

Sylvie is selfish and impulsive and reactive and has never met anything she couldn't destroy. The princess is a princess and was a princess and was always going to act like a princess, no matter how much they both tried to forget that. She deserves to be the one trapped for once.

But Sylvie doesn't. She can't. Because in the exact same moment the princess gave her every excuse to condemn her, she also forced her to acknowledge how desperately and breathlessly she cares about her.

So, she runs. She's faster than the princess so as they bolt down the tunnel metal digs into her wrist—a constant reminder of how deeply Sylvie's been betrayed—and the lantern light flickers in and out of view, but she keeps running anyway because she *needs* to hate the princess. She won't be able to do that if she gets her caught.

Sylvie destroys everything.

(She can never help herself)

But if she destroys the princess too, then she won't get to tell herself that for once, someone else screwed her over more.

The princess gasps the occasional direction as they run, but she's otherwise silent. Sylvie lets that fuel her. The princess kidnapped and threatened her, but she hasn't even attempted to apologize for it yet.

(Their screaming lungs don't matter, she just needs an excuse to be mad)

They burst through a wooden door up towards the night sky and she wants to keep running, but all at once, she stills. There are *stars in the sky*. There are *her stars* in the sky. Sylvie cranes her neck as far back as she can manage and stares. She breathes in the night air.

It's hard to know how desperately you're missing something you can't remember, but all at once, she understands. It was a blessing to forget. If she could remember feeling like this, she never would have settled for anything less.

"Sylvie." Something tugs at her wrist, ruining the moment. "We need to go. If we find transport before they notify anyone, we—"

She turns to face her. "Where's the key?"

"That's not…" The princess looks away. "I don't—"

"Give me the fucking key!" Sylvie practically growls as she tackles her to the ground. The lantern hits the earth and sputters before going out, but panic doesn't grip her. There are *stars in the sky*.

"Sylvie!" the princess squirms beneath her, trying to escape. She should know better. She's the one who bound them together.

Sylvie grabs her free wrist with her shackled one to force both of her arms to the ground. She straddles the princess's lower body to keep it pinned as she begins to frantically pat her down. "Where's the fucking key!"

"I don't have it!" the princess sobs, pressing her cheek to the grass to avoid looking at her. "I got rid of it!"

"Why would you do that!"

"Because I knew you'd ask!"

Sylvie gives up on questioning. She runs her hand down the princess's side. She needs to move quickly. She can't condemn her to an eternity of unending slumber, but she won't do any more to help her escape either.

The princess squeezes her eyes shut. "Sylvie!" she gasps. "Sylvie, please! I'm…" her breathing's ragged with tears. "I promise I don't have it. I'd give it to you if—stop it!" she shrieks. "Please!"

Sylvie freezes. She pulls her hand away. "That's not fair."

"I know," the princess blubbers. "I know, I—"

"That's not what I'm doing."

"I know. I know. But I really don't have it. I really—"

Sylvie rolls off her. She drags them both to their feet.

"We can wish it off once we're out of Rosenly, okay?" the princess rambles. "Somewhere with stars. Then we can—"

"We'll wish it off here. No point not using them now."

"That's…" the princess chews at her lip. It's disgusting. "I won't," she says. "I won't, I need to—I've barely left the castle! I need to… you can't wish. I can. And I'm not wishing for that until we're out of the kingdom."

"I could keep you here," she threatens again. "Don't need your light anymore."

"I know," the princess says. "I know, I'm… I'm sorry. This is my only option."

Sylvie stares at her. She steps closer, then leans until she can practically feel each hair on the princess's skin. "I hate you for this," she hisses, forcing her to meet her eye. "I was maybe the only person in the entire kingdom who genuinely liked you, and now I'm going to hate you forever."

"I know," the princess whispers. "I'm sorry. I have to."

Sylvie waits another beat to see if she'll break, but she doesn't. She sighs, moving away.

"Do you have matches?"

"I… yes?"

"Don't forget the lantern, then," Sylvie mutters. "We'll have to bribe our way into the back of a transport cart. I can push down your starlight long enough to keep you from being recognizable, but sitting up front'll be too risky. I'm not spending hours sitting in darkness for you."

"Okay," the princess bends to grab it. "Okay. Thank you," she hesitates. "I'm sorry, Sylvie. I'm really, really—"

She tugs at her arm. "Let's go."

The Last Princess of Rosenly

The last princess of Rosenly has never been a particularly good person, but she never needed to be.

She was pretty, once.

(before Sylvie knew her)

She's tragically beautiful, now.

(In ways Sylvie doesn't care about)

But she's never been good at anything but pretending. So, she drags them to the nearest road, flags down cart after cart, and allows Sylvie to do all the talking.

She needs her. She wouldn't have known the right things to say. She'll only be alive for a few more weeks, so surely she deserves to be selfish.

(Sylvie told her she should be)

But as they sit crouched in the back of a transport cart, wedged between crates of fruit they've been threatened to not even consider touching, she can't help but wish she was actually as good as all the princesses in all her stories purport to be.

(Maybe that's why she's the only one who won't get a happy ending)

As Sylvie keeps her eyes pointedly locked on the flickering lantern and positions herself as far from the princess as their joined arms will allow, all she wants is to be the kind of princess worth wanting to save.

But she isn't. She left. She ran.

(Princesses worthy of saving rarely get to stop anything at all)

She tries to speak a few times, but every hushed "Sylvie" or "sorry"—the words begin to blur together—is met with a swift kick to her leg and a rushed "shh", so by the time they emerge from the cart hours later into the waiting sunlight

of unfamiliar lands, the tension between them's only grown.
Sylvie hands the driver a single gold piece from the princess's
bag and marches off into town, though the princess knows she
must be just as directionless as she is here. She rushes to
match Sylvie's pace, careful to keep her cuffed wrist pointed
towards the earth. Her cloak conceals the metal, but just
barely. Her parents *will* come looking for her. She doesn't
need to give anyone an excuse to stop them and ask questions.

"Sylvie."

Sylvie picks up her pace and she has to jog to keep up.

"Sylvie!" She catches the fingers on her trapped hand.
Finally, Sylvie stops and turns.

And the princess realizes she hasn't a clue what she's
supposed to say next. "I umm… I wanted to…"

"We're finding somewhere to stay," Sylvie informs
her. "We're buying enough food for the day then we're
finding somewhere to stay and we're not coming out until we
can wish our way out of this tonight, understood?"

"I…" she nods. "Yes, but—"

"Then you're paying me. Half your money, because
it's not like I can just go back to Rosenly with half the fucking
kingdom probably looking for me already."

"I wrote a note!" she remembers. "I said it wasn't
your fault!"

Sylvie just stares. "You wrote a *note*."

"Yes! So—"

"You're giving me half your money because a note
means fucking nothing, then we're parting ways in the
morning and I never have to see you again, deal?"

"That's…" She hears her voice tremble. "I can't…
you said you'd come with me."

"And you didn't trust me to do that!"

She can feel heads turn to watch them. Sylvie closes her eyes and takes a deep breath.

"We're finding somewhere to stay," she repeats. "We're buying food for the day, we're staying until tomorrow morning, and then I'm leaving. This isn't a debate."

"Okay," she says. "That's… okay."

Sylvie turns again and continues onward towards town.

"I'm sorry, Sylvie. I'm really, really sorry."

When she doesn't respond, the princess tries to convince herself she just didn't hear her.

Sylvie

She's proud to find the princess's tears don't affect her anymore.

They find a room for rent near the heart of town—Sylvie chooses it. It'll make it easier to lose her when they part ways—and Sylvie instantly does everything she can to signal that she's in no mood for talking, so instead, the princess wastes Sylvie's next few hours of freedom on listening to her trying and failing to conceal her sniffling. There's nowhere to escape to, so Sylvie drags them both into the bedroom, throws a pillow over her ears, and rests in an actual bed for the first time in over a month, hopeful that when she awakes, the princess will have at least gotten a handle on the crying.

She hasn't.

"I'm going back home," the princess whispers once Sylvie makes the mistake of sitting back up. "I'm... you don't have to come, but I thought you should know—"

"Bullshit."

"I am," she insists. "It'd be better for the kingdom. I never should have... if you tell me where your constellation's located, I could even—"

She freezes. "Don't you fucking dare."

The princess frowns. "I don't—"

"Do you think I'm an idiot?"

"That's not—"

"You think I'm seriously going to believe you went from desperately wanting to run away last night to—"

"Last night I didn't think I'd have to be alone!" The princess's eyes widen at the sound of her own outburst, then she sighs, deflating against the headboard. "I'm sorry," she says. It's practically all she's been saying. "I shouldn't have...

I don't know how to be a person, Sylvie. No one bothered to teach me. I'm not... I'll go back. I'm going to be miserable either way, so I might as well... I just wanted you to know. If you ever want to come back to Rosenly, I'll make sure no one thinks any of this was your fault, okay? I swear."

Now that she's immune to her crying, Sylvie's finally able to recognize a manipulation tactic when she sees one.

She won't cave, though. She gave the princess her chance at freedom. She doesn't owe her anything more.

(She's supposed to think she owes her less than that)

(She can never help herself)

"Might as well leave me more of the money, then," Sylvie says. "Since you won't be needing it."

"Okay," the princess says. And, "Of course." And "I'm sorry."

Sylvie doesn't respond. For a while she thinks that's genuinely won her silence, but then a couple of hours later, the princess says, "you tried to kill me, Sylvie. I'm... I get why you're mad, but if this is the last time I see you, you could at least—"

"I didn't know you yet," she stops her. "You knew me. You... I'd literally already promised I'd come!"

"I couldn't be sure, though. I couldn't—"

Sylvie has destroyed everything. Sylvie has been trusted by no one. Sylvie will not allow this girl to hurt her again. "I'm not risking my freedom for someone who trusts me so little that they couldn't believe I'd follow through on a plan *I* came up with."

"But—"

She rolls over to face her, but only for a moment. "I might've tried to kill you, but I wasn't going to. You knew from the very beginning I wasn't going to. It was an impersonal step of a stupid last-ditch plan," she pauses, but she doesn't feel better yet. "I cared about you though, Strella. I was going to ruin fucking everything for you. And you threatened to torture me the moment I even *thought* about pushing back against something you wanted to take from me."

"I'm sorry," she repeats uselessly.

"I don't forgive you." Sylvie rolls back over, stares through the glass ceiling, and waits for darkness to arrive.

The Last Princess of Rosenly

Nightfall comes both too early and too late.

Sylvie keeps them trapped in the bedroom for as long as physically possible, returning there instantly and wordlessly whenever either of them needs to get up for anything. The last princess of Rosenly knows it's because she's desperate to use the façade of rest to ignore her, so she lets her. Whenever she tries to talk, she ruins things further.

(Princesses worthy of saving rarely get to stop anything at all)

Sylvie hates her. She will always hate her. There's nothing she can do to rectify that, so she might as well spend their last few conscious hours together avoiding as much conflict as possible.

(Princesses worthy of saving rarely get to stop anything at all)

Sylvie pretends to fall asleep—or maybe she actually does—hours before sunset, but when the first stars begin dotting the sky, her eyes instantly fly open.

She thought she'd known how Sylvie wore happiness before seeing her beneath starlight, but she'd been wrong. The stars completely transform her. Her posture somehow relaxes and gains new life simultaneously, her eyes almost brighten, and she doesn't smile so much as she loses the ability to frown.

And because of one stupid, selfish decision, she might never be able to return to her own stars ever again.

The last princess of Rosenly watches her adapt to the night sky and tries to breathe in as much of the memory as she can, but Sylvie's expression settles back into annoyance far too quickly. She swings herself off the bed, forcing the princess to awkwardly clamber after her.

"Are we—"

Sylvie doesn't even let her finish. "Let's go."

It's been years since the princess last saw starlight, but as she stands beneath it, she feels nothing at all. She's expecting a terror or a yearning or a kinship. Her parents were half convinced the stars existed purely to antagonize her, after all. But as Sylvie pulls the princess past town and into an isolated clearing, all she sees is light.

It's almost a comfort, this obvious confirmation that she never spoke to the stars in the first place. At least this way, her death will be slightly less a personal failure.

Once Sylvie decides they've traveled far enough, she crosses her legs and sits down. Grass tickles the underside of the princess's thighs. She can't remember the last time she sat in it.

(Maybe she never has)

Sylvie holds out her palms expectedly and waits for the princess to lace their fingers together.

(She tries to not focus on this being the last time she'll get to do that)

"Okay," the princess breathes. "What do—"

"It's easier to move something than get rid of it," Sylvie says. "Think 'I wish these cuffs fell off both of our wrists' and only that."

"Okay," the princess chews at her lips. "Of course. I wish—"

"Are you going to be able to mean it?" Sylvie interrupts.

"What?"

"Are you going to actually mean it? I'm not wasting my time—"

"I—yes," the princess decides. "Of course. I—"

"You seemed pretty desperate to force me to stay with you last night."

"But you don't want to," she says. "So of course I'd... you deserve to be happy, Sylvie. I know that."

"Do you?"

The princess sighs. "Let's see." She says the phrase aloud exactly once then switches to mentally chanting it. She hadn't even considered it might not work but now, worry seizes her. There are actual stars in the sky this time, but it feels like it's taking longer.

Maybe she can't mean it. Maybe she's too selfish.

(It's her birthright)

(If it doesn't work, Sylvie will never forgive her)

All at once, the cuffs slide through their wrists. They become fully solid again just in time to fall to the ground with a single, quiet thud.

The last princess of Rosenly forces herself to release Sylvie's hands. "Well," she stands to go. "I guess this is umm..."

Sylvie catches her arm. "Sit," she says. "We're not done."

"But—"

"I wish no one would be able to recognize me as a wish or princess until I tell them who I am."

The princess frowns. "Why would—"

"When you inevitably refuse to go back home, I'm not letting you drag me down with you when someone identifies you."

She licks her lips. "I'm really going back, Sylvie."

"Well then, this'll make it easier to get there," Sylvie shrugs. "Might not even work. It's a bigger ask."

She holds out her hands. The princess takes them.

(For the last time)

"I wish no one would be able to recognize me as a wish or princess until I tell them who I am."

When this wish works, it almost destroys her. Sylvie's face goes from pinched and angry to content. When she opens her eyes again, she takes a moment to survey the sky before her gaze finds the princess. Her eyes aren't kind—Sylvie is not the kind of person who offers kind eyes to strangers, yet she still threw it away once she'd finally decided to give them to her—but they're not angry either. They're just confused.

The last princess of Rosenly considers leaving them that way, but she can't let herself. She's taken too much from Sylvie.

"It's umm... it's me, Sylvie," she says. "Strella. Estrella. The umm... the princess. Of—"

Instantly, Sylvie snaps back to anger. She practically throws the princess's hands against the earth.

"Sorry," she can't help but whisper.

Sylvie brushes her palms off against her pants, pushes herself to her feet, then starts marching back towards town. "See you in the morning," she mutters.

But she won't. The princess has already decided. When she wakes, Sylvie will have to remember she hates her all over again, and the princess can't do that to either of them.

So, the last princess of Rosenly allows herself to watch her until she's little more than a speck in the distance. Her first friend, seventeen years too late. The only citizen of Rosenly whose hatred has every right to be sharp and personal and pointed.

Her last friend too, but the last princess of Rosenly only has a few weeks left anyhow. She will learn to cope.

She wanders town aimlessly until she's certain Sylvie must have fallen asleep. Then and only then, does she let herself begin the journey home.

Sylvie

She's not surprised when she wakes to find the princess nowhere in the bedroom.

She heard her come in at some point during the night, but she's fairly certain she never even approached the bed. That made sense. It was predictable.

Rosenly's princess is and always has been a coward, after all. It was how she tricked Sylvie into pitying her enough to pretend to care in the first place.

But then, she leaves the bedroom and finds the entirety of the princess's satchel poured out on the kitchen table, the satchel itself sitting empty on the chair. And a note. There's a note.

She approaches it cautiously, as if it might gain sentience and attack her at any moment. But it doesn't. It's only a piece of paper. It's nowhere near as significant as it feels like it should be.

She considers tossing it away without reading it, but she doesn't. She's almost certain it'll be another empty apology, but she doesn't want to have to spend the rest of her life wondering.

She flips it over. It contains only two words, but not the ones she was expecting.

Thank you.

This is every single coin and gem the princess brought with them. It must be. Of course a princess who's spent her entire life safely confined to castle walls would've never even stopped to consider that she might need at least something to buy her way back to them.

It's stupid. It's selfless and ridiculous and so, so stupid.

Sylvie grabs the satchel and swipes the table's entire contents into it. She doesn't let herself examine the strange feeling in her gut. She doesn't let herself worry about how the princess is planning on getting back home.

She certainly doesn't let herself consider what might happen once she gets there.

This is the happy ending. Sylvie is free, the princess got to experience a few moments of living like someone unburdened by a curse, and now, she's chosen to return to Rosenly of her own accord to presumably let Sylvie's constellation put her to sleep for the rest of eternity.

This is the ending where almost no one at all has to get hurt.

She throws the satchel over her shoulder, walks out the door to try and plan where to go next, and tells herself she'll be able to ignore that feeling in her gut forever.

(She can never help herself)

Sylvie

Sylvie ends up in a tavern not because she's desperate to drink, but because it seems the loudest place to be.

She is an expert at escaping herself, and right now, she wants nothing more than to stop carrying the burden of thought. She's forgotten, though, all the ways that the princess is a little too much like her. She's been at the bar for less than an hour before she learns that the princess hasn't gone nearly as far as Sylvie had hoped.

(Or dreaded)

There is apparently a girl outside trading drinks for kisses then pouring them out onto the earth. She only knows one person who would do that.

"Hey!" Sylvie bursts back outside to find the princess wedged between the wall and a tall, bearded man who's clearly already drunk more than his fair share. His words slur as he shouts unintelligibly at her. His hands slip down her waist. The princess squirms and breathes and winces.

She shouldn't intervene. The princess clearly wants this. She's evidently gotten it into her head that a kiss might be able to save her after all.

But she's trembling. She's trembling and Sylvie's supposed to hate her and this is clearly what she wants, but she's trembling.

"Hey!" Sylvie moves closer.

(She just can't help herself)

She pounds a fist against the man's back. "What the fuck do you think you're doing!"

He turns to Sylvie with blurred, unfocused eyes. "Said she wants a kiss," he says. " 'm just—"

"Yeah? Did she say that meant you could fucking touch her?" She tugs at the princess's arm. "Come on," she demands. "This is ridiculous. It—"

"He didn't kiss me yet!" the princess exclaims.

She just blinks at her. "You seriously think—"

"He didn't kiss me!"

Sylvie sighs. She turns back to the man. "Alright, kiss her, then leave her alone."

He moves to grab at her again, but Sylvie steps in the way. "Hands behind your back this time. Or I'll go tell the barkeep you're groping malnourished teenagers right outside the entrance to their establishment."

The man pouts. "But—"

"Arms behind your fucking back."

He complies. He leans forward to kiss the princess. She wipes the back of her hand against her lips once it's done.

Sylvie doesn't know what she's supposed to be doing next.

"Alright then," she nods. "You," she points to the man. "Go get some water or something, and you," she nods at the princess. "Stop doing whatever this is. If..." she winces. "If you need money, or something—"

"I don't."

"Alright then," she turns to go, but the man grabs her arm.

Because he's tall and drunk and at least twice her size, and she antagonized him.

(She can never help herself)

"Hey," the man squints at her. "Don't recognize you, do I? Are you new to—"

"I don't see why that's any of your—"

"Aye!" The drunk waves over a group of other men waiting by the fountain. Men that are evidently completely fine with leaving their friend alone to assault a dying teen. Sylvie knows the princess isn't recognizable, but from what she remembers from the few hazy seconds where she hadn't known who she was, the wish messes with a viewer's memory, not their actual perception. She'd looked like herself, just slightly blurrier wherever starlight should be. But these men don't care about her age or her failing body. Maybe because they've already assaulted her themselves. "She's new, isn't she?"

He hasn't let go of her arm. "I don't see why that's any of your—"

"You a weaver?" One of his friends asks.

She freezes.

"They're looking for one in Rosenly. There's a reward. Supposed to bring anyone who might be one to an outpost to get checked out."

"I'm not a fucking weaver!"

"Still new to town, though. Maybe we should test it."

"How the fuck—"

"Lance!" One of the men disappears into the bar to do who knows what.

The drunk still hasn't let go of her arm. Sylvie considers pointing out that the princess is also new to town, but she knows it won't do anything. They're not targeting her because she's new, they're targeting her because she won't let them stick their tongues down her throat. If anything, reminding them that the princess also needs to be 'tested' will just give them another excuse to touch her again.

Sylvie might be pissed, but she's never going to let that happen.

The princess doesn't care about her, though. She stands staring at the confrontation for a moment, but she's already fading into the growing crowd. She's going to run.

Sylvie's only in this mess because she was stupid enough to try and help her again, but she's going to run.

(If she could turn back time, she still would have interrupted)

(She can never help herself)

The man who ran into the bar emerges with the barkeep in toe. "Lance says we can use the cellar!" he says. "Lock her up for a few hours and see if she cracks."

Sylvie freezes. "That's not—even if I was a weaver, that's not a crime!"

"Course not," the man shrugs. "And if you are, I'm sure you'd be fine accompanying us to the border to let them check you out."

She sighs. She forces her expression to remain blank. "If I'm letting you waste an hour—"

"Two."

"*An hour*," she repeats. "Of my life, I better be getting free drinks out of it after."

That seems to calm them, slightly. It's aligned her more with them. Someone actually begins to cheer. They turn towards the barkeep, waiting for his verdict.

He nods. "You've got yourself a deal."

Sylvie weighs her options. Both choices are bound to end in disaster, but maybe she can be quiet enough that no one will hear her scream. Maybe the cellar isn't as void of light as they think.

Both choices will end in disaster, but at least this one will give her a bit of time to stall. If she's handed over to the King and Queen, she knows she'll eventually break and give too much. It's her only option.

She nods. "Let's go then."

As she's escorted back into the bar, the princess doesn't even bother looking at her. Sylvie takes another breath, rolls her shoulders back, and lets herself be dragged towards damnation.

The Last Princess of Rosenly

The last princess of Rosenly forgets how to speak.

She can feel the imprints of hands on her waist and stomach and hips and chest. She's always known people in the kissing line could sometimes take it too far but now, that feels like nothing. These hands seared into her skin. She can't escape them. She never wants to be touched again.

And so, when Sylvie reappears, instead of seizing the opportunity to finally do something to even begin to make things right between them, she forgets how to speak. She just watches.

(Princesses worthy of saving rarely get to stop anything at all)

By the time she comes to her senses and rushes into the bar, Sylvie's already vanished.

"I'm new too!" she declares to no one in particular.

All heads turn to face her. She's used to all heads turning to face her, but with her skin still freshly seared, she suddenly wants to shrink down enough to disappear from sight. She doesn't let herself. She can't.

"I'm..." She takes a deep breath. "I'm new too," she repeats. "I'd rather be tested now. I have... plans. Later."

The barkeep stares at her. "If you're offering yourself up, I doubt—"

"I don't want to have to waste time getting questioned again later." She extends her wrists towards him.

(She hopes he doesn't decide to actually touch her)

"Take me away," she says. "Please."

The barkeep still looks perplexed, but he removes a keyring from his belt and escorts her to the cellar regardless. She begins to panic as they approach it. She knows how quickly darkness can tear Sylvie apart. She can't let him open the door and see that.

Luckily, though, the cellar's down a long, dark flight of stairs. She hears no screaming from the bottom of it, but if anything, that terrifies her more.

Last time, Sylvie was screaming five minutes in. Last time, silence meant something far, far worse.

"Thank you, then!" She tries to smile cheerily. "I'll be… see you in an hour!"

She sprints down the steps as quickly as her legs will carry her.

Sylvie

Sylvie Castell will never get any wishes, but if she had one, she'd wish to undo.

The what is irrelevant.

(Though she knows exactly where she'd begin)

The when doesn't matter.

(Though she knows exactly when she'd go first)

Sylvie Castell is the kind of person who catches others' smiles between her teeth just to tear them to shreds, so if she had one wish, she'd wish to undo.

Something.

Anything.

Everything.

She'd beg each and every star to rewrite her story entirely and then make the same mistakes all over again because she can never help herself, but at least for a few moments, she'd no longer be a fuck up.

(A Sylvie who can decide will always be a Sylvie who decides wrong)

But Sylvie Castell will never get any wishes, so she sits in the darkness, bites down on the side of her hand, and tries to trace through the myriad of mistakes that led her to here.

By the time the princess rushes into the cellar, her ears are ringing, her vision's blurry, and she can feel blood dripping down her chin. She doesn't need a clear head or vision to recognize her, though. Strella is the only person she's ever known to glow in darkness.

Sylvie presses her palms against the dirt, scrambling backward until she collides with an immovable crate. "No," she whispers through clenched teeth.

She thought insanity might make her forget, but she remembers last time so clearly it might as well have been seconds ago. "You can't—I can't—"

Strella's abruptly kneeling directly in front of her. Sylvie tries to move further, but she has nowhere to go. She's going to scare her. She's going to *hurt* her.

(She can never help herself)

"Stay away!" she says. "You need to—"

"Shhh," the princess takes her hands, both whole and bloodied. "We need to be quiet, remember? Can you do that, Sylvie? You were already doing such a good job."

She momentarily manages to obey, but only because of the shock of the princess's skin—the princess's *starlight*—against her fingers. She can't let herself demand more. She craves it.

"I don't..." she quivers. "You shouldn't—"

"Shhh," Strella pulls her into a hug and all at once, there are stars pressing against her arms and shoulder and back. "It's okay," she whispers. "You're okay. You've lasted more than an hour before, remember? You're going to be fine."

She won't be. She can barely form a coherent thought and she's *touching her* and she's not supposed to be anywhere near her.

It's only when Strella shifts to press more exposed skin against hers that Sylvie realizes she's doing it on purpose. Strella pulls away, but she doesn't let go of Sylvie's arms

(she knows she never will)

(she knows she has to)

"You can control it, right?" Strella searches her eyes. "Can you move it so—"

Sylvie shakes her head. "I won't," she says. "I'm not—"

"Sylvie," Strella squeezes her arms. "It's okay. That's why I'm—"

"I'm not going to touch you!"

Strella bows forward. She presses her forehead to Sylvie's. "It's okay," she runs a star-speckled hand down her arm. Sylvie hates how quickly it calms her. "It's okay. I'll stop you if it's too much. I trust you."

(She doesn't)

"You don't."

"I do," Strella insists. "I did. I made one stupid split-second mistake, but I do."

Sylvie watches her. Her head screams. Her eyes water.

"Please, Sylvie."

She takes a deep, shuddering breath. "You'll tell me to stop," she whispers.

Strella nods. "I will."

"And I will. The second you tell me to. I'm—"

"I know."

She pulls starlight.

She traces it through blood and up bones. She wraps it around nerves. She finds every shimmering speck and pulls it out from sleeves and fabric until there's no starlight left on the princess beyond her bright, glowing arms. Sylvie lets herself breathe. It's slightly easier now. She meets Strella's eye.

"Okay?" she checks.

Strella nods, but all her attention's on her hands. "Okay."

She frowns. "Are you—"

"I'm okay, Sylvie," she forces a smile. "You were right. I don't feel a thing. Promise."

She starts to reach for her wrist, then reconsiders. "Can I—"

"Whatever you need."

She squeezes her eyes shut against a sudden spike in the ringing. "I don't need to touch you," she says. "I'm… It'd still be fine, if you just touched me. It'd—"

"It's okay," Strella offers up both palms. "I trust you."

"I don't," she whispers. "I'm… I'll ruin it. I'm—"

(She can never help herself)

Strella wraps one of Sylvie's hands around her wrist for her. "Then I'll just trust you enough for both of us."

She starts with her forehead again, pressing Strella's palm against it. It works quicker this time, with the light all pulled together. She waits for her mind to clear before slowly guiding Strella's hand down her neck and across her shoulders. She's going to be okay. As long as she has this, she'll be okay. She closes her eyes and cycles Strella's palm across her entire body twice before she's ready to open them again.

She's met by Strella's wide, glowing eyes.

"They wanted to get more guards into the castle," she says.

"What?"

Sylvie winces. "I need to be talking," she says.

"Okay."

"I also need you to not be talking."

"O—" Strella catches herself. She nods.

"They wanted to get more guards into the castle," she repeats. "Ideally they'd hire more and we'd have constellation members first in line, but even if they didn't, we've spent years getting enough on staff. We wanted to have more weavers in the building so they'd have more of a chance of wishing you away the moment they found you. Did it work?"

she risks asking. "Did they… After I attacked you. Did they increase the guard?"

Strella hesitates. "Can I talk now?"

"Obviously."

"Yeah, then," she nods. "Almost right away."

Sylvie can't tell if she's telling the truth or lying to appease her, but her head's buzzing too severely for her to dwell on that.

"You should've taken money with you," she says, slowly running Strella's hand down her leg. "That was stupid."

"I was trying to apologize."

She rolls her eyes. "A good apology wouldn't have forced me to worry about you."

"You worried?"

"Of course I did."

Strella licks her lips. "I don't think I'm going back, Sylvie," she admits. "I tried to, but I couldn't…"

"So you decided to let drunk assholes grope you instead?"

She shouldn't have said it. Strella shivers. She doesn't pull away though, so after briefly pausing to see if she's about to object, Sylvie keeps directing her arm.

"It felt better than doing nothing," Strella eventually whispers.

Sylvie nods exactly once. "You don't owe me this," she forces herself to admit. "You shouldn't… I'll be fine," she says, as she continues tracing her palm. "You don't—"

Strella frowns. "You got in trouble trying to help me."

"I got in trouble because I never know when to mind my own fucking business," she corrects. "That had nothing to do with you. But even if it did, you still wouldn't—"

"Sylvie," she stops her. "Please let me fix something, okay?"

She swallows. "Okay."

The Last Princess of Rosenly

She should feel guiltier for hoping the hour'll never end than she does.

Sylvie might seem calm, but she knows even if the starlight's soothing her completely, she must still be at least a little terrified. She should want to get it over with as quickly as possible.

But she doesn't. Because she isn't alone.

The moment she realized she couldn't make herself return to Rosenly the princess had resigned herself to spending the rest of her life—no matter how short that might be—in solitude, but right now she's with Sylvie and they're both soft and quiet and gentle. She knows it won't last. She knows the moment they're both safe again, Sylvie will remember she hates her and she'll have to leave forever. But for now, she's content prolonging her own solitude.

The hour has to end, though, so as the door creaks open, Sylvie quickly sends her starlight shooting back across her skin. She doesn't know if it'll do anything—the wish she made the night before seems to keep anyone from noticing the starlight at all—but she doesn't stop her. It's easier to pretend it doesn't exist when some of it's beneath her shirt.

Sylvie glances at her injured palm as they approach the stairs and the princess instantly takes it. They need to conceal the wound. She's not ready to let her go.

(Princesses worthy of saving rarely get to stop anything at all)

When they exit the cellar Sylvie keeps their fingers entwined and Strella knows it's just to hide any proof she had to muffle her screams, but she lets herself pretend it means just as much to Sylvie as it does to her.

(Hope is a very hard thing to kill in a princess, after all)

Sylvie must forget that she bartered for free drink, because she moves straight for the door.

"Aye!" One of the men at the bar jeers. Strella freezes. She runs her tongue along her teeth.

(Sylvie brushes a single finger across her knuckles, but maybe she's just imagining it)

"Thought we weren't allowed to touch 'er!" he nods at their clasped hands.

Sylvie rolls her eyes. "Some of us aren't twice her age. Shouldn't have locked her alone in a room with me for an hour if you didn't want me taking her home with me."

This time, she knows Sylvie's touch is real. She forces herself to exhale.

Sylvie nods once at the man then pulls her through the doors.

"Am I?" Sylvie drops her voice once they're back in the sun.

The princess has no idea what she could possibly be referring to. "I... what?"

"Am I taking you home with me?"

She freezes. She tells herself she's misunderstood. She tries to shove it down.

(Hope is a very hard thing to kill in a princess, after all)

"Strella?" Sylvie prompts, pulling her further from the tavern before stopping to face her directly.

"That's not... You don't have to," she says. "You don't owe me that either."

Sylvie rolls her eyes. "Bold of you to assume I'd ever let myself owe anyone anything."

She wants to say yes. She's *desperate* to say yes. "It really wasn't bad for me, Sylvie. I don't want you to forgive me because you think I made some kind of sacrifice for you, because that wasn't—"

"I'm forgiving you because you would have," Sylvie stops her. "I don't want you making sacrifices for me, but I'm forgiving you because I didn't for a second even consider that you wouldn't, okay? And…" she sighs. "People don't tend to trust me. That's… I think that was the only thing I was actually upset about. That you didn't."

"It was a mistake," she whispers.

"I know that now," Sylvie nods. "And… I mean, I did try to kill you. Technically. If we're keeping score." She holds out her other hand. "We've got a bit over three weeks left, right? Wanna go make them less shitty together?"

She grins. She hugs her.

She doesn't even hesitate.

Stars

Sylvie

They keep moving.

Sylvie decides it's best to not risk crossing another border, but if they've already sent guards after them, they can't stay this close to Rosenly's.

Strella's never gotten to see the world. She only has three weeks left to show it to her. But they waste one of them constantly on the road, slowly moving further and further away until they and Rosenly are nearly an entire kingdom apart. Strella suggests conserving money for wherever Sylvie's planning on going next, but she won't let her. Instead of renting a room, they rent an entire cottage, with a garden all its own and a ceiling wide enough to let in endless starlight.

She can't show Strella the world. She might not look like herself to anyone but Sylvie, but they're still two strange girls around just the right age. They can't let themselves be recognizable enough to cause suspicions. They take turns going into the market sparingly and spend the rest hidden away. The least they deserve is a prison with a view.

Still, they try to make the best of it. They spend their days walking forests and their nights at the outskirts of any festivity either hears the slightest of rumours about. She can't show Strella the world, but she can at least help her experience what it might have been like to live within it.

When they're down to their final ten days, Strella tries to get rid of her.

They're toasting water over the first truly awfully burnt loaf of bread they've tried to make themselves when she abruptly puts down her glass, averts her eyes, and says,

"You could go now, if you want."

Sylvie forces herself to roll her eyes. "What? Trying to keep this all to yourself?" She sweeps an arm over their monstrosity.

"I'm serious, Sylvie."

It hits her, like most things do, directly in the gut. They'd been good, she'd thought. Better than good. There was no grand strife or conflict or trauma to bond them, they'd just been two girls enjoying each other's company, trying to ignore the looming end. "Sick of me already?" She tries to joke. And it *sounds* like a joke, but Strella knows her far too well for that.

"You know I'm not," Strella says, because she's all too aware that Sylvie might not. "But I'm going to die, Sylvie. Soon."

"All the more reason to stay. It's just a few more days."

"That's not..." Strella sighs. She pinches her brow. "I'm going to die, Sylvie. You don't want to be there for that. I'm not trapping you again."

"Who said I didn't?"

Strella exhales. "It's hard," she picks at her fingers, "to care about something you know will die. It's—"

"Bold of you to assume caring about you was ever any kind of choice."

"Sylvie."

"*Strella.*" She rips off a piece of bread and chucks it at her. "People die," she agrees. "Each and every one of them. By your logic, no one should ever risk caring about anyone at all."

"But I have less time," she argues. "That makes it harder to—"

"That makes it harder to even consider spending a second without you." She lets her arm fall back to the table, allowing her fingers to brush against Strella's. "Let me stay," she says.

"With your own family, you didn't even—"

Sylvie freezes.

And Strella's Strella, so of course she notices. "I'm sorry, I shouldn't have… Do you know where they are? You could go to them. Or we could—"

"They wouldn't want me to."

And Strella's Strella, so she laughs as if that's the most ridiculous thing she's ever heard. "Why would they—"

She stands too quickly. "Stop asking!"

(She can never help herself)

Her chair's knocked off balance. It clatters against the wooden floor.

Strella's face morphs with understanding. It's too late. She's given herself away. Now, Strella really will force her to leave.

(She can never help herself)

"It umm… He was hurt?" she tries to justify it.

(She can't)

"He was hurt and he was sick and I was scared and I could *see* him wishing so I—my father took the blame. And they sent him back *broken*."

Slowly, Strella stands. She carefully rounds the table, arms raised in surrender.

(Because she's scared of her, again)

(Sylvie can never help herself)

"Did they… They blamed you for that?" Strella asks. "They wouldn't let you go with them even though you were only—"

"I was old enough to know better."

"You weren't—"

"I was old enough to know it'd be safer for everyone if I stayed behind."

"You *saved someone*, Sylvie," the princess lies.

"Who might not have needed me to. And I destroyed my own family in the process." She takes a deep breath. She picks at her nails. "I'm reckless Strella," she whispers.

(She can never help herself)

"I'm reckless and reactive and... I think I might destroy you too. If I had longer than ten days. I did it twice already, so maybe—"

"That's why you volunteered to sacrifice yourself," she realizes. "Not because of a mistake you made at nine, it was the one you made at—"

"It was all of them, actually. I'm—I get selfish and impulsive and—anything that touches me eventually ends up destroyed."

Strella stares at her. She takes another, minuscule step. "I think I really do need you to stay then, actually."

Sylvie laughs. "Because I'm going to destroy you?"

"Because you think you will," she corrects. "Because you think the worst thing you've ever done is saved someone. Twice. Three times, maybe. If I can count more than once." She takes another step. She's impossibly close. Sylvie can feel the heat of her skin. "You don't destroy things, Sylvie. You save them."

"I save the *wrong* things."

Strella shakes her head. "You don't get to take on the weight of everyone else's decisions just because you can loosely connect them to some of your own. It's a bit egotistical, actually. You're not really all that important."

Sylvie snorts.

"I'll be dead in less than two weeks," Strella looks straight at her. "There is nothing you can do to destroy me, my destruction started when you were an infant, okay? Which means this time, the only thing you can possibly carry with you is the saving. Stay," she says. "Please." She holds out her arms, waiting for her to choose the embrace. "I'll beg, if you need me to."

Sylvie rolls her eyes before burying herself against her shoulder. "I was never the one who wanted to leave, stupid."

Strella

She's never felt more unburdened than she does as she's dying. Her every step feels lighter. Her every breath feels easier. Maybe because the stars are also affecting her in some invisible, unquantifiable way. Maybe because as her body continues to shut down, there's less of her to carry around in the first place. Perhaps it's that for the first time in her life, she feels entirely known by someone. Sylvie's carrying some of her too now, so that might explain the lightness.

But deep down she knows it's not the stars or her flesh or even Sylvie, it's that for the first time in her life, Strella is nothing at all. Not a kingdom's hope nor downfall nor future queen nor doomed princess. Not a mouth nor a body nor beautiful nor tragic. She is just a person. A person who's dying, but she's had seventeen years to come to terms with that part. It's selfish to have left. She's abandoned the mess made just for her. She would make the same decision over and over again.

(Princesses worthy of saving rarely get to stop anything at all)

So of course, when she's down to her final four days, the skies decide to ruin things for her once again.

"Get inside." Sylvie was only supposed to go to the market for milk and eggs, but as she sprints down the trail, she's carrying neither.

Strella drops the book she's been reading on the porch step.

She's been enjoying that a lot more now.

(Reading)

(Sunlight)

"What—"

"Get the fuck inside." Sylvie skids to a halt. "Sorry," she says. "Just—" She gestures wildly at the door, so Strella rushes to unlock it. Sylvie scrambles in after her, slams it shut, then begins pulling furniture up against it.

Strella stares. "What's—"

"They're here."

She frowns. "My parents' guards?"

"No, your actual fucking parents."

She almost falls over at that, but luckily, she's had years of practice pretending she doesn't want to. "Why—"

"Someone told them we're here. There's no time to leave, they're already on their way. Someone recognized us."

"But how—I don't even look like me!"

"We're too strange girls using Rosenly dialects who abruptly just appeared to hide in the woods, Strella. Not like it'd take much to figure it out." Sylvie stops. Slowly, she turns to face her. "Promise I'll stop taking this out on you for no reason once we're safe," she says.

Strella laughs. "Don't worry. I'm tougher than I look."

"You are exactly as tough as you look," Sylvie corrects. "Stars and bones and bloody lips. Anyone who's ever thought otherwise was clearly an idiot."

"I can help barricade," she offers.

Sylvie hesitates. "You also can barely stand for more than a minute at a time right now. Go toughly block off the windows."

"It could be a good thing, you know!" Strella calls as she works on the one in the kitchen. "I can explain I came of my own consent, now that they're here! That I wanted to leave!"

"Are they going to listen when you tell them that? Or just drag you back home to let strangers kiss you on your literal deathbed?"

She doesn't respond. They both know the answer.

"Alright then," Sylvie appears around the corner. "Then you can tell them all about how much you consented to be here. Through an extremely barricaded—" She freezes. Her eyes lock on something just above the princess's head and widen.

Strella frowns. "What—"

All at once, beams of light begin shooting up from her skin. At first she thinks they've come to take her early, but her own starlight remains untouched. This is something different. This is something new. She stares, rolling her wrist and watching the strings of light follow it. "Are those—"

"You can see them?"

"They are, then," she realizes.

(Hope is a very hard thing to kill in a princess, after all)

"But… it's the middle of the day. Aren't they not supposed to—"

"They're also not supposed to look like that." Sylvie moves closer. She wisps her fingers through a few strands of light.

"What does that mean?"

"I think," Sylvie says slowly. "I think it means you were right. I think you must've talked to them."

"But I didn't—I don't even know what I'm wishing for!"

Sylvie grins. She locks their fingers together. "Wanna find out?"

Sylvie

She's never granted a wish without knowing the wisher's intent before. It isn't supposed to be possible.

But then, neither are wishes visible beneath the light of day. Neither are wishes that look anything like this at all.

Maybe it's because it's Strella and she *is* a wish, maybe it's because it's Strella and she's dying, or maybe it's simply because it's Strella and Sylvie knows with her entire being that whatever she is wishing for, she wants as well. Whatever the reason, when she attempts to move the strings, they weave themselves together. She knits each end tight and snug, then right as she begins to despair that she has nothing to weave her tapestry into, strands begin to rush down from the sky as well.

She laughs. She's giddy. She's everything. She is the only weaver who has ever gotten to handle this much starlight at once.

When she opens her eyes again, there's been no evident change. Strella stares at her. She stares back.

"Did it not—"

A giant crack sounds just beyond the kitchen window. They rush to it just in time to see the flowers beneath it grow to giant, gnarly, twisting vines. In a matter of seconds, they envelop the walls, leaving nothing bare but a small gap above the ceiling for light to trickle through.

"*Stars.*" Sylvie stares. She's simultaneously exhausted and invigorated. "Did that—"

"They'll let you pass through," Strella breaks through her stupor.

"They'll…" She turns to face her. "I'm sorry, what?"

Strella's cheeks colour. "They told me. They'll, you can pass through, if we need anything. They'll part for you. They won't let anyone else in."

She gapes. "The *stars* told you that."

"They... they still won't save me, Sylvie. They... they'll keep us guarded until then, though. They—"

"You're talking to the fucking *stars*?"

Strella begins to grin. "Yeah, I... I suppose I am."

Sylvie laughs. She throws her arms around Strella's waist, lifts her off her toes, and they spin together beneath a sun-streaked sky.

Nonymous

Sylvie

Strella

It's a strange sort of comfort, having her parents so near yet unable to touch her.

(They wouldn't want to anyway)

(They never did)

They yell at first, of course. They come at the vines with soldiers and machetes and canons, but they barely leave even a scratch. When they give up, they are almost parents.

They cry. They beg. They tell her how desperately they want to get to see her, just one last time.

(Her mother looks at her even more sparingly than her father does)

She coaxes the vines to part exactly once to allow them to look at her, but once she does, neither are brave enough to meet her eye.

(She takes Sylvie's face between her palms once the vines reclose)

(She needs to remember that she is more than tragedy)

Eventually, they give up. They give in. When they allow Sylvie to move freely on the second last day of her life, she's not naive enough to believe it's truly because they've given up, but at least they're pretending to understand.

(That's all she's ever wanted from them)

They even apologize, on her last day.

(That's everything she's ever wanted from them)

They promise to be better. To fix things. She doesn't know if she can trust that, but she'll be dead soon, so she allows herself enough selfishness to believe that they might.

As night creeps in, she loses her ability to walk entirely. The vines thicken further. It's a strange sort of comfort to have her parents so near yet unable to touch her, but in her final moments, she doesn't want the world to be any more complicated than her and death and stars and Sylvie.

(It's strange to remember she used to think each of those one of the most complicated things of all)

Sylvie stokes the fire then climbs up onto the bed to lie down beside her. Strella isn't cold, but Sylvie keeps convincing herself she must be. She wants to give her a way to feel useful.

"Hey," Sylvie whispers. "Still up?"

"Until the end."

"Morbid," she accuses.

"Yes." Strella rolls onto her side, curling up to face her better. Perhaps if she compresses her stars just tightly enough, she'll be able to win them both a few more minutes of exactly this.

"I'm sorry I couldn't fall in love with you," Sylvie whispers.

She kicks her shin.

She knows it must be beyond weak, but Sylvie at least has the decency to pretend to hiss.

"Don't apologize for my favourite thing about you."

"*That's* your favourite thing?"

She shrugs. "Guess you don't have many other glowing qualities."

"Bitch," Sylvie mutters.

"Asshole."

She feels Sylvie shift down to lie with her, and for a fraction of a second, she sees it. The flicker of sadness in her eyes. "I need you to go, Sylvie."

She frowns. "I… What?"

"I need…" She squeezes her hand. Searches for the words. "I wanted you here as long as possible," she says. "You did that. You were. But now… The entire world has only known me as dying, even when it wasn't actually happening yet. I don't want you to too."

"I won't."

"Please," she whispers. "Just…"

She watches Sylvie's eyes water, but she doesn't take it back.

(Dying girls are allowed to be selfish)

(Sylvie told her she should be)

"I don't want to abandon you," Sylvie whispers.

"You won't be. You didn't. You'll just be a room away. I just… I don't want you to see it. Please."

(Princesses worthy of saving rarely get to stop anything at all)

"Okay," Sylvie says. "Of course."

"I'll miss you!" she calls after her. They're not the right words, but she doesn't know any strong enough. "You were… everything."

"And a pain in the ass sometimes?"

She grins. "Those were my favourite bits."

She gives in to the pressure at her eyelids and allows them to fall shut. "Go," she whispers. "I want to feel exactly like this, okay?"

She feels the mattress shift as Sylvie stands. She clasps a firm, calloused hand around her shoulder. "See you in the skies, Strella," she says.

She smiles. "Follow you forever."

The hand's removed. Sylvie's footsteps retreat. The door's closed.

She counts to one hundred before opening her eyes to face the sky head-on.

Eighteen years were a long time. She's realized that all too late. But at least for a couple of weeks—at least with her—she'd been able to live quietly enough to live off of for eternity.

Strella

Sylvie

She sits at the kitchen table and busies herself with stirring a cup of tea that's already long past appetising.

There's singing outside, somewhere in the distance. Mourning.

She's glad Strella didn't have to hear any of that.

When she hears glass shattering in the bedroom, she doesn't let herself wonder if it's her body leaving for good or simply the vines breaking the glass to ease the transition. Strella didn't want her thinking about her death, so she doesn't allow herself to.

(She can help herself)

Instead, she looks toward the future. She plans next steps.

Once the princess is gone, the vines will recede. She might be arrested again, but perhaps a bit of Strella's hope has rubbed off on her, because she truly thinks the King and Queen might keep their word this time.

Promises to a broken kingdom are one thing. Ones made to a dying child feel so much less fragile.

And, she's the one who's left the cottage enough to see them cry. Maybe they were smart enough to realize what they were losing after all.

When she's not arrested, she'll move north. Strella made her promise to. She laughs slightly to herself when she realizes she was perhaps not the only one to realize the weight of a parting promise.

She's been manipulated. She shakes her head in amazement and welcomes it.

She'll move north and she'll find her family and she'll let herself believe at least a little, that they might not hate her after all. She'll move north and she'll find her family and she'll be strong enough that if they do, she'll know that doesn't have to mean everyone else will. She'll fall apart for a few days then pull herself back together and move on to the next potentially wonderful thing.

(She can help herself)

If they take her back, though—*when* they take her back—she'll tell them of a girl with impossibly bright eyes and a maniacal smile. Of bloodied lips and steadied hands and terrible, inedible soups. She'll tell them of how she made Sylvie a little gentler and the world a little kinder and the skies themselves brighter than they've ever felt before, not because of the light beneath her skin, but the person who laid beyond it. She'll tell them that her world was never as good as it was with Strella in it, but that maybe, she's taught her to believe that her after will not have to destroy her.

She'll tell them of the girl who changed her life. Who was everything. Who—

"Shit," she drops the spoon. Tea splatters onto the table. "Shit, shit, shit—" She scrambles to her feet. She rushes to the door.

Because, like most things, she's realized it moments too late.

She loves her.

Nonymous

Nonymous

Soulmates

Sylvie

"Strella!"

By the time she reaches the bedroom, she's already too late.

Strella's unconscious form hovers above the bed, tendrils of light slowly dragging her toward the broken ceiling.

"Shit!" She hits the wall. "Shit, this can't—"

She tries to jump for her, but it's useless. She's too high.

She stares at the sky.

Sylvie Castell will never get any wishes, but if she had one, she'd wish to save her. Sylvie Castell will never get any wishes, but Strella wasn't supposed to be able to physically see her wishes either.

They've broken the rules for her once. They can do it again.

"Put her down!" she screams. "Let me—She doesn't want to go! Let her go!"

Strella moves higher and higher still. Sylvie attempts to pull a dresser closer to climb it, but it's useless.

"Let her—" A vine bursts in through the window. It snakes across the wall beside the bed, disappearing into the clouds. Sylvie stares. Sylvie cries. And then, she wraps a bedsheet around her fists to protect them from thorns and begins to climb.

Sylvie

When she finally surpasses Strella in height, she's still just out of reach. She manages to grab hold of her foot and attempts to pull, but she won't budge. So, Sylvie moves higher. She'll need to jump. She'll have to jump.

(She can help her)

She tries to plan out how to do it. She knows Strella hates kissing, but this one is necessary. She won't mind.

(She might mind)

Her heart hammers. Strella rises. She'll pass the ceiling if Sylvie doesn't move quickly.

And so, she squeezes her eyes shut, purses her lips, and hurls herself off the vine.

Her lips engulf the entire tip of Strella's nose before they both fall back onto the bed.

Strella

She's hoping the next thing she sees will be the ground. Once the princess might have thought she'd be okay with simply fading away, but Strella can't accept that now. Now that she's gotten a taste of life, she wants to spend her eternity witnessing every possible moment of it.

But when she does snap into consciousness, all she can hear is ragged breathing. She smells nothing but sweat.

Something on her face is very, very, damp.

She forces her eyelids open. One at a time. "I... Sylvie?"

She's lying beside her, panting so rapidly that Strella momentarily worries she's not the only one dying. Then, Sylvie's head jerks up, she stares at her, and then tackles her back into the mattress.

Strella giggles, squirming against the sudden embrace.

(Not out of it, though)

(She could stay in this one forever)

"What—" she starts. "How—" She sits up so suddenly that it almost knocks Sylvie off the bed. "You're in love with me," she whispers. "Stars, I—"

Sylvie bursts into laughter. "Of course I'm not!"

She feels her shoulders relax, but only for a moment. "Then how... Why is my nose wet?" It's too distracting for her to focus on any of the other nonsensical things around her.

"I kissed you."

"On the nose?"

"Apparently so."

"But why... How—You're sure you're not in love with me?"

Sylvie rolls her eyes. She crosses her legs. She takes Strella's hand. "Yes," she says. "But I umm... Maybe I... It's true love's kiss. Not *in* true love's kiss. And I think at some point I started to umm—"

"It didn't work, though," she remembers. "We kissed before. It—"

"I wasn't made to love you, Strella," Sylvie says. "I think if I was, I would've at least known... I thought you were a bitch, actually. For a really, really long time."

"Thanks?"

"But," she continues. "I think that means... It wasn't a choice either. I don't remember choosing. I probably wouldn't have. I don't think it's destiny or desperation or... I think I care about you because I got to know you too well to *not* care about you."

"That's..." Strella's heart swells. "You love me," she whispers.

"Shut up! No I don't!"

"I thought... Sylvie you were literally just explaining that you did. Enough to anchor me to the ground."

"Oh," she blushes. "Right."

Strella laughs. She throws her arms around her neck. "You *love* me," she sings. "You could barely even admit we were friends and now you *love* me."

"It would've had to be mutual," Sylvie grumbles. "For it to work."

She laughs again. She tries to stand. It works. She takes a step towards the door then holds out a hand to bring Sylvie with her.

"Ready to face the rest of our lives?"

"Stars, no," she groans.

The princess grins. "Too late. There's no stopping it now."

Nonymous

About the Author

Alex (any pronouns, feel free to talk about them behind their back at will, they're impossible to mispronoun) is a queer, disabled almost-23 year old who's published 20 queer disabled YA books so far because they're wildly self-centered. They write across genres (though there's almost always *at least* a vague allusion to a fairytale in there somewhere)

Message alexnonymouswrites@gmail.com to get added to their email list and get updates on future releases, early reading opportunities, and to vote on upcoming genres!

Content Warnings: nonconsensual touch/kissing, swearing, negative self talk, death & dying, subconscious/unintentional self-harm, blood, imprisonment, panic/anxiety attacks